NANCY JOHN
Secret Love

Silhouette Desire

Originally Published by Silhouette Books
division of
Harlequin Enterprises Ltd.

First published in Great Britain in 1986 by Silhouette Books, 15–16 Brook's Mews, London W1A 1DR

© Nancy John 1986

Silhouette, Silhouette Desire and Colophon are Trade Marks of Harlequin Enterprises B.V.

ISBN 0 373 50486 1

22–1286

Printed and bound in Great Britain by Cox & Wyman Ltd, Reading

"Why The Sigh?"

Quinn murmured.

"Because I'm feeling happy."

"Strange logic!" His hands roved her back, sliding down the ridge of her spine. "Does that mean that you smile when you're feeling sad?"

"Sometimes."

"Problem. How do I read you when you smile at me?"

"You'll just have to wonder." Paula lifted her face so she could touch her lips to the tip of his nose. "When I was a small girl I used to burst into floods of tears when something especially nice happened."

"Not anymore?"

"Well . . . not lately."

"Pity! It would have given me the chance to kiss your tears away. Like this . . ." Quinn softly pressed his lips to each of her eyes in turn, lingering caressingly. Then his mouth skimmed across her cheek, searching out every curve and hollow, tasting the silken texture of her skin. The tip of his tongue probed her ear until Paula shivered with the exquisite sensation.

"I suppose," he whispered, "in your contrary way you're shivering because you're warm?"

"Something like that."

NANCY JOHN

has been a full-time writer since 1964. She lives to travel and research the backgrounds of her novels, whose settings she describes vividly. She and her husband of thirty years make their country home in Sussex, England, where they pursue their love of nature in the romantically beautiful English countryside.

Other Silhouette Books by Nancy John

Silhouette Desire

Night with a Stranger

Silhouette Special Edition

So Many Tomorrows
Web of Passion
Summer Rhapsody
Never too Late
Dream of Yesterday
Champagne Nights
Rendezvous
The Moongate Wish

One

Ow!'' muttered Paula Chamberlain, clapping a hand to her suddenly prickling left eye. "Of all the darnedest luck.''

It could hardly have happened at a more inconvenient moment. She was crossing from the beach to her hotel after an early morning swim in the blissfully warm water of the Mediterranean.

The stinging grew worse as Paula pushed through the revolving door of the Hôtel de la Plage and made her way across the elegant lobby to the bank of elevators. One of the gilt cages stood waiting with its gate open. Stepping inside, she blinked away her streaming tears to focus on the panel of buttons.

"Let me," said a deep voice, as a man entered behind her. He spoke in English. "Which floor do you want?" Then, before Paula could answer, "Having trouble? Something in your eye?"

"A grain of sand, I guess. I want the sixth floor, please."

"Right. But just let me take a look at your eye first."

"Thank you, but no. I'll be fine when I get to my room."

"The sooner it comes out, the better," he said decisively. "Now, hold still for me."

Paula gave up protesting as deft fingers touched her cheek. He seemed to know what he was doing, she thought thankfully, as he rolled down her lower eyelid gently but firmly.

"Aha! An eyelash. Hang on, this isn't going to hurt."

Paula felt just a faint brushing across her eye. Then mercifully the pain was gone. As her vision cleared she found herself looking at the white handkerchief he held up for her inspection. On the tip lay a curving dark lash. Paula let her glance travel upward and met a pair of vividly blue eyes that glinted with good humor and intelligence.

"Thanks a lot," she said. "It must have come loose in the water." She was suddenly self-conscious about her skimpy apparel, just a terry-cloth beach wrap over her swimsuit. She put up her hands to scoop back the thick dark curls that were clinging wetly to her forehead.

"Does the eye still hurt?" he inquired solicitously.

"Oh, it's nothing now. That was neat, the way you whipped out the lash in a couple of seconds. Are you a doctor or something?"

"Not even a something. I learned the trick at my mother's knee." He grinned as he added, "She had another effective cure for minor mishaps. It always seemed to work like a charm."

"What was that?"

"To kiss the hurt better. Let's put it to the test."

He acted swiftly, catching her unaware. Resting his hands lightly on her shoulders, he leaned forward to touch his lips softly to the corner of her eye. Paula allowed it to happen, amused by his nerve. Then, as he drew back from her, dropping his hands, she experienced the strangest feeling. Despite its lightheartedness, there had been a sensual quality about that feathery kiss. It was the first time she'd had any physical contact with a man since the death of her husband ten months previously.

"Well, did it work?" he queried. "Or had I better try again?"

"Don't push your luck." To conceal her embarrassment, Paula quickly turned to the control panel and stabbed the button for the sixth floor. But before the gate could close, the elevator was invaded by a troop of people—part of a tour, presumably, because they were all talking together animatedly in a language that Paula didn't recognize. She and her rescuer were pushed apart.

As the elevator began its smooth ascent he mouthed something at her from five feet away. Paula smiled and shook her head, unable to lip-read. He gave a rueful shrug and continued looking at her with an intent eye.

Still shaken by her reaction to his kiss, Paula moved fractionally so that the disturbing eye contact was broken. From behind the shield of someone's shoulder she was able to conceal her interest in him. He was outstandingly attractive, with the easy self-confidence an awareness of good looks can give to a man. She liked his strongly carved features, the determined jaw, the generous mouth and the nose that was set just a tad aslant and gave him a faintly whimsical look. His hair was a rich chestnut color, glinting with reddish highlights. It was lush and springy and looking somewhat tousled at the moment, as if he'd been walking outside in the frisky breeze blowing off the sea. Contrasted against his open-necked white shirt, his throat looked deeply bronzed, and beneath the fine cotton was a wonderful breadth of muscled shoulders.

Paula guiltily peeled her gaze away and saw with a mixture of relief and regret that the elevator had reached her floor. Easing through the throng, she glanced back and gave her helpful stranger a parting smile of thanks. Instantly his blue eyes locked with hers. They posed a question that she didn't choose to answer.

Walking down the hall to her room, Paula gave a happy sigh. She felt certain she'd see more of him. He knew her floor, and it wouldn't be difficult for him to track her down. If he didn't make contact again, it would mean he wasn't that interested. Which, on the basis of the looks he'd given her, Paula couldn't believe.

In her room, Paula showered and dressed after first calling room service for a breakfast of orange juice, croissants and coffee. She preferred not to meet any of her colleagues from Chamberlain's right now; she would see quite enough of them over the next few days. Instead, she wanted to be alone to luxuriate in her thoughts.

These past ten months she hadn't lacked male attention. But she hadn't been in any hurry to start dating, and up until now no man had sparked her interest. Not that this morning's encounter would lead to anything, of course, beyond the mildest flirtation. But, all at once, the thought of a lighthearted interlude was appealing...an intriguing extra dimension to the pleasure of the job that had brought her to this South of France resort.

At precisely six minutes before ten, Paula left her room and started down the hall again. Now she looked like a smart, poised, self-confident woman. She wore a a cream linen skirt and jacket teamed with an apricot blouse, the outfit nicely setting off her summer tan and the suede-brown of her eyes. For business Paula always wore her nearly black hair neatly pinned up in a chignon, to leave no doubt in men's minds about her professional competence.

Down in the hotel lobby, Paula at once spotted her colleagues sitting together beneath one of the huge gilt mirrors. The three men were paying court to the petite figure of Lady Chamberlain, the firm's head and Paula's mother-in-law. Chicly garbed in blue silk, her pale silver hair wound in a braid on the crown of her head, her small feet in custom-made patent shoes, she looked as fragile as rare porcelain. How false appearances could be! Behind the facade of poise and charm she was as tough as steel and ruthless, too. As Paula knew, to her cost. Widowed at forty-two, Arabel Chamberlain had, in the past twenty years, expanded the modest antiques and fine arts auction house she'd inherited from her husband into the world-renowned business it was today.

Any warmth in her smile of greeting to Paula was negated by the ice in her voice.

"Here comes our sleepyhead at last."

Paula matched the smile with one that was equally insincere. "Sleepyhead, nothing! I was out swimming before the rest of you were even awake."

"Really?" Finely penciled eyebrows lifted delicately. "So that's what delayed you, dear."

Paula had no need to check her watch. With a boss like Arabel Chamberlain she had to avoid making elementary mistakes like bad timekeeping.

"You told us ten o'clock, Lady C. There's still a couple of minutes to go."

Paula greeted the three men of the party with a friendly word. It was working alongside such nice people that helped counterbalance the major disadvantage that went with her job at Chamberlain's. Their grins indicated that,

as usual, they'd been entertained by this exchange of un-
pleasantries with her mother-in-law.

"Let's go, then," Lady C. said impatiently, rising to her
feet. "The car will be waiting." As they started moving
toward the exit, she halted and released a pained sigh.
"The Sylvester's people are coming this way. Oh, well,
we'd better get the civilities over and done with. I really
think they might have had the courtesy not to stay at the
same hotel."

Paula was about to point out that the same could equally
well be said of their own party, but she choked back the
words. Her attention was riveted on the tallest of the five
men approaching them across the spacious lobby. Her
helpful stranger from the elevator! Paula immediately
guessed who he must be, because she already knew his four
companions. Quinn Barclay, a man who trailed a reputation in the art world as a tough negotiator who needed to
be treated with wary respect. Some eight or nine years
previously, Chamberlain's rival firm of Sylvester's had sent
him to their New York office as an assistant auctioneer. He
had stormed through the ranks and now headed Sylvester's entire American operation. Quinn Barclay must often
have been in London in recent years, she knew, but until
this morning their paths had never happened to cross.

The "civilities" went unheard by Paula. It was just too
cruel that the bright promise of her chance encounter in the
elevator should be abruptly ended like this. Quinn Barclay was the man whom Lady Chamberlain despised above
all others for what she termed his cheap, huckster methods.

His crime against Arabel could hardly have been worse.
He had dented her pride and made her look like a fool. The
previous year, when an important Spanish collection of
medieval paintings had come on the auction market, she'd

boasted that Chamberlain's had the contract all sewn up. At the last minute, however, Quinn had flown to Madrid and somehow secured the sale for Sylvester's. At no time would Arabel have been content to see her widowed daughter-in-law associate with Quinn Barclay. But just now, when both auction houses were locked in competition for the art world sale of the century, he would be totally beyond the pale as far as she was concerned.

Paula was jerked from her gloomy thoughts by her mother-in-law's voice.

"Paula, my dear," she drawled. "Introductions are superfluous, I think. Except that you may never have met Quinn Barclay before." She spoke the name with distaste.

"No, I don't think I have." Paula gave a polite nod around the group, which included the portly chairman of Sylvester's, Lionel Fairhurst. Then her eyes wavered toward Quinn, to be instantly pinned by his questioning gaze. She answered with a tiny shake of her head. She felt the supple warmth of his hand as it closed around hers, and, unmistakably, a sensuous feathering of his fingertip in the center of her palm that brought hot color stealing to her cheeks.

"How do you do, Mrs. Chamberlain? I know about you by reputation, of course. When it comes to ceramics and antique silverware, you're way out front."

"It's very kind of you to say so, Mr. Barclay."

"You're too modest, Paula." Lady C. said it more as a rebuke than a compliment. She never missed a chance to insist that Chamberlain's had the best possible lineup of talent at their command.

Lionel Fairhurst said genially, "Well, Lady C., so at last we're going to get our hands on all the goodies that old Charles Webberley accumulated over the years. One of us, that is. The battle of the giants, eh, what? Who'll be the lucky winner, I wonder.''

"Chamberlain's, naturally. Unless, that is..." Lady C. cast a contemptuous glare in Quinn Barclay's direction. "Unless you're contemplating methods I myself would never stoop to."

Quinn was totally unruffled. He just looked amused. "Isn't the auction business in the same combat zone as love and war, Lady Chamberlain?"

"That remark shows the gulf between us, Mr. Barclay," she responded frostily. "To you this is mere commerce. To me, handling beautiful works of art is a privileged calling."

Quinn inclined his head. "A matter of definition, I think. When it comes to the bottom line, we're all in the game to turn a profit, aren't we?"

"Speak for yourself, Mr. Barclay," she threw back with unveiled hostility.

Lionel Fairhurst coughed discreetly. "I suppose we'd better get moving. No doubt we shall keep bumping into one another at the Webberley villa."

In the limousine, as it left the busy resort town and headed for the quiet hills, Lady C. remarked sourly from her corner seat, "Quinn Barclay is unspeakably brash and uncouth. He's a stain on our profession."

"Oh, come now, Arabel," protested Sidney Crowe. Having been with Chamberlain's even before Lady C. had come into the picture, he was privileged to use her first name. "We all know that you're prejudiced where Quinn Barclay is concerned."

"Me? Prejudiced!" She looked affronted.

Sidney smiled equably. "I wouldn't expect you to like the young man. But the fact that he bested you over the

Spanish sale last year doesn't of itself make him a villain."

She dismissed that with a flick of her hand. "It surprises me to hear you taking his side, Sidney."

"It isn't a matter of taking sides, Arabel. Simply of trying to be fair to him."

"Fair? That man wouldn't even know the meaning of the word."

Paula listened to their exchanges with a feeling of disquiet. Sidney's defense of Quinn wasn't helping any to reduce the temperature of Lady C.'s dislike of him. Paula half wished that Quinn hadn't needled Lady C. and made her even more antagonistic toward him. But she'd hate him to have taken her blistering put-downs without hitting back.

The Webberley villa, high on a rocky promontory, was a white marble palace, reminding Paula of a tiered wedding cake. It was set amid exquisite formal gardens. The Chamberlain's team was the first to arrive. A manservant admitted them to a lofty, pillared hallway that was crammed with priceless treasures.

Charles Webberley, having made a vast fortune from shipbuilding, had retired immediately after World War II at the early age of forty-five. Thereafter, right to the end of his life, he had devoted himself to collecting works of art and displaying them around him in his Riviera home. Now Charles Webberley was dead and there were no heirs. He had never married, and each and every one of the transient ladies in his life had been generously rewarded at the time of their parting. Under the terms of his will everything was to be sold for the benefit of various charities; and these had formed a united front to make sure of raising the maximum sum possible for their funds. Hence the keen competition of the two great auction houses.

Chamberlain's and Sylvester's would bid against each other for the opportunity to handle the prestigious Webberley sale. Each would pare its percentages to the bone and dangle the promise of getting better prices under the hammer than its rival.

"Good morning, ladies and gentlemen." A dark-suited figure had appeared from nowhere, greeting them with grave decorum. "I was the late Mr. Webberley's personal secretary. Adrian Harper. The staff here have been instructed to afford you every facility, and you'll find refreshments laid out in the small morning room."

The staff, it became obvious as the Chamberlain's team split up to inspect their own specialist interests, included numerous alert security guards. After a quick look around the principal rooms, Paula gravitated to the dining salon, where the bulk of the silver collection was located. Her task was to estimate the total potential. Detailed cataloging would be carried out by other staff if and when Chamberlain's won the sale.

She worked steadily, making notes. From time to time the hushed silence was broken by footsteps as a guard paced by the open doorway. Paula spent several pleasant minutes inspecting a superb pair of Regency wine coolers decorated with acanthus leaves that stood on fluted feet. She had never seen better specimens. These alone would fetch a small fortune. She handled them lovingly, like a sculptor his marble, running her fingertips over the smooth surface.

"Magnificent, aren't they?"

At the first syllable Paula recognized Quinn Barclay's voice. Straightening, she turned slowly to face him. There was no one else in sight. Ridiculously, it made her feel nervous to be alone with this man.

"What are you doing here?" she asked.

"My job."

"But paintings are your thing. The ones in this room don't amount to very much."

Quinn gave her a slow smile. "I really came to talk to you, Paula."

"Well, please go away again. I'm extremely busy."

"Too bad! So will we meet later? How about a drink this evening?"

"Sorry, I don't think that would be a good idea."

"No? I think it's a great idea. Even better, let me take you to dinner."

Paula heard footsteps again. But it was only the guard. He glanced in at them without interest, and passed by.

"Please be sensible," she begged Quinn.

A small frown creased his brow. "We need to get together and talk, Paula. Aside from anything else, I'm intrigued to know why you put on an act that we'd never met before."

"Well, we hadn't. Not really. It was nice of you to do the Good Samaritan bit in the elevator, but I've said thank you. So that's the end of it."

"Why not call it the beginning, instead?"

Although they were standing a good four feet apart, Quinn's face seemed to fill her vision. She could discern tiny darker flecks in his intense blue irises as his eyes narrowed in puzzlement, see each separate laugh line that radiated from their outer corners. She could almost feel the smooth texture of the skin that stretched over prominent cheekbones. A bright beam of sunlight, reflected from a silver platter, turned his chestnut hair to the color of maple leaves in autumn.

"What do you say, Paula?" he pressed, when she didn't speak.

"I've already given you my answer. No to a drink. No to dinner."

"It would be just as easy to say yes."

She shook her head, crushing down temptation. Quinn Barclay was just an attractive man she'd encountered in quirky circumstances and who had caught her interest. Almost at once, she'd discovered that he had to be a no-go area. Bad luck, but it didn't measure up to a catastrophe. Any further contact with Quinn would lead to problems, and problems were something she could do without.

"Why don't you go and get on with your work, and let me get on with mine?" she said in a brusque tone.

Quinn felt exasperated. Her reluctance was impossible to understand. It wasn't his style to be pushy; dammit, he'd never needed to be. But if he weren't now, he risked losing the chance of getting to know this woman who interested him more than anyone he'd met in a very long time. He'd never forgive himself if he let that happen.

"Come on, Paula. Give me one good reason why we shouldn't meet for a drink."

"There'd be no point in it."

Voices could be heard approaching through the adjoining anteroom. Arabel Chamberlain was exercising her authoritative charm on the secretary.

"If you'd be so kind, Mr. Harper, it will be so much easier when my staff come to catalog the collection if you could have your people rearrange it into separate sections."

"She's taking victory for granted," said Quinn, with an amused twist of his lips. "The battle hasn't even started yet." Then quickly, "We'll talk later, Paula."

"There's nothing for us to talk about."

"I can't believe you mean that." The look in his eyes caused a warm thrill to fountain up through her body.

The approaching voices were almost at the door now. Paula somehow got a grip on herself. As she turned away and bent to inspect the wine coolers once more, she murmured over her shoulder, "Thanks for not giving away that we'd met before. But let's leave it there, please."

She didn't see Quinn shake his head in dissent. When Lady Chamberlain and the secretary entered the dining salon, he was apparently absorbed in inspecting a landscape by a minor Flemish painter, his pen poised over his jotting pad.

Two

It was an amazing sight. Three huge African elephants were cavorting in the shallow waves near the beach, squealing with delight. The circus was in town. Paula had noticed the bills announcing it as she'd left the hotel for her swim. Now, from her viewpoint on one of the floats anchored in the bay, she watched their antics with amusement.

At this early hour there was already a number of bathers, but mostly they kept close inshore. Paula, after ten minutes of energetic swimming, was content to rest on the float and enjoy the beauty of the morning. The sea sparkled all around her, and the small town glowed in the sunshine. In the hills above, screened from the town by conifer woods, stood the Webberley villa. Its hundred windows glittered like diamonds, as if proudly advertising the hoard of fantastic treasures within.

Letting her gaze return to sea level, Paula noticed that a swimmer was making a beeline for the float. Arms flashed and a head bobbed as he approached at a fast crawl. Her breath caught in her throat as she recognized him. Damn Quinn Barclay! What a time and place he'd picked to get her alone.

For an instant she was tempted to plunge back into the sea and swim away, but it would only postpone the showdown he seemed intent on having.

"Hi!" he greeted her cheerfully, grasping a rope. "Beautiful morning, isn't it?"

"Lovely," she agreed. But her cool tone was meant to make it clear that his arrival hadn't added anything to her enjoyment.

With a quick thrust of his powerful arms, Quinn heaved himself onto the float. Rivulets of water streamed off his splendid body. He was magnificently proportioned, Paula noted, the wide shoulders tapering to a trim waist. She tore her gaze away from the lean hips that were encased in dark crimson trunks. Quinn made himself comfortable, leaning back on his elbows with his long legs stretched in front of him.

"I presume," Paula said with a frown, "it isn't a coincidence that we're both on this float?"

Quinn's mouth quirked. "Would you believe me if I said it was?"

"Hardly."

"I thought if I joined you on your early morning swim, we could spend some time alone together without getting interrupted by your mother-in-law."

"I don't know why you bothered. I thought I'd made myself clear yesterday."

"That's exactly what you didn't do, Paula. I can't figure out why you suddenly went cold on me when you discovered who I was. I think I'm entitled to an explanation."

"Entitled? Because you removed a lash from my eye?"

"Forget entitled. Just do me a favor, will you? There has to be a reason for your sudden about-face, and I'd appreciate knowing what it is."

It was impossible to tell him the truth. Paula shrugged impatiently. "I'd have said it was obvious. You and I . . . we're competitors, for heaven's sake."

"Which doesn't make us enemies. I'll be going all out with the rest of my team to win the Webberley sale for Sylvester's. So will you and your people. But there's life beyond the Webberley sale." Quinn shifted, bringing up his knees and clutching his arms around them. The movement sent a fluid ripple of muscle under his taut, tanned skin. "I'll make you an offer, Paula Chamberlain. If I misread the interest I saw in your eyes, come right out and say so and I'll accept it. I won't like it, but I'll accept it. Tell me to get lost and I'll dive back in the sea this minute."

He was offering her an easy way out, but Paula couldn't take it. That would be too unfair, too hurtful. The silence lengthened while she stared down at the sun-spangled water. She could feel Quinn watching her, his gaze on her face. The tension between them was electric.

"No, Quinn, you didn't misread the situation," she said in a low voice. "Yesterday, in the elevator, I decided that you were a very attractive man. But if it hadn't been for that lash in my eye you and I would merely have smiled at each other and maybe traded a few flippancies. Then we'd have gone our separate ways."

"If? I don't go for ifs, Paula. I deal in facts. You did have a lash in your eye. Something sparked between us in those moments in the elevator."

"I've said so, haven't I? But afterward, when I discovered who you were..."

"You were fazed. I'll forgive you for that, as an instant reaction. You felt embarrassed, I guess, and you didn't want to have to do any explaining to the others. But we've been properly introduced now. So aren't you carrying this keep-your-distance routine a bit too far?"

"You just don't understand. Suppose I agreed to have dinner with you or whatever, and my mother-in-law got to hear of it. What would she think?"

"Does that matter? You aren't scared of her, are you?"

Paula dodged a direct answer. "She'd have every right to feel angry."

"Like hell she would! But justification is beside the point with Arabel Chamberlain. She disapproves of me, of course...."

"You can say that again."

"Arabel Chamberlain disapproves of me." When he grinned, Quinn's eyes became even more intensely blue. "It gets up the old girl's nose that I use the techniques of a salesman. Or rather, that I don't mind admitting that I do. Trading in the arts is little different from trading in any other commodity. It's a commercial enterprise. But that boss of yours likes to cloak her business manipulations. She acts as if she's motivated purely by altruism. She projects herself as a gracious and noble patron of the fine arts."

"I shouldn't be listening to this," Paula said uncomfortably.

"I'm telling you nothing you didn't know already."

Paula was silent. Quinn had made a shrewd analysis of Arabel Chamberlain's character. The hairs on his forearm, already dried by the hot sun, glinted golden amber against his skin. She glanced away.

"I'd like an answer, Paula. I'm still lost for a reason why it's such a crime that you and I should spend some time together."

Paula took a moment considering how to reply. "I just don't think it's worth stirring up a lot of bother so you and I can see each other a couple of times."

"Is that all you give us? A couple of times?"

"What else? You'll be in New York and I'll be in London."

"There's a way around every problem if you try hard enough. A new relationship is a new beginning. It has infinite potential." Quinn laughed ruefully. "Now that I think of it, Lionel Fairhurst won't exactly dance for joy about our seeing each other, either. But we can't let his feelings and Lady C.'s stop us. It's the way we view the situation ourselves that counts, Paula. A question of our personal integrity. Seeing me isn't going to undermine your loyalty to Chamberlain's, is it?"

"No, but . . ."

"The same goes for me. So let's be open about what we feel. Let's have breakfast together. Let's meet for dinner this evening. Other people can make what they like of it. but you and I know that neither of us is stepping an inch out of line."

Paula shook her head. "No, Quinn."

"Scared I'll manage to pry Chamberlain's secrets out of you?"

"Huh! You'd be lucky."

"You'd need more than luck to get Sylvester's secrets out of me. So how about it, Paula?"

She hesitated, vastly tempted. But she dared not take a risk with Lady Chamberlain's anger. Arabel had a mean streak. If she discovered a liaison between her daughter-in-law and Quinn Barclay, a man she loathed passionately, she might be enraged enough to put her venom to deadly effect. Were it only her job in jeopardy, Paula thought with a sigh, she'd say to hell with such considerations. But Lady C. held a gun to her head.

"I'm asking you again, Paula." His voice was soft, coaxing. "And I'll keep on asking. Let's face this thing head-on."

"I'm sorry," she said candidly. "I truly am sorry, Quinn. But I can't agree to see you."

A sudden trumpeting noise from the shore snapped the thread of tension between them. The circus elephants were being led, protesting, from their water frolic. Paula gave a nervous laugh.

"Time I was getting back." She stood up so quickly that the float rocked beneath her. Instantly Quinn was on his feet to steady her. For a few seconds they stood utterly still, looking into each other's eyes. Only his hands touched her, lightly, at the waist. But Paula felt breathless, and her heart thudded wildly. It couldn't have felt more unnerving if he'd held her in an intimate embrace. Then she broke away from his hold, stood poised for an instant and made a clean dive into the crystal blue water.

"I'll give you a count of twenty," Quinn shouted when she surfaced.

Watching her slender body strike for shore, with ripples caressing her smooth, honeyed skin and her dark hair floating out behind her, Quinn felt a painful yearning. Somehow he had to overcome Paula's curious reluctance about their relationship and give it time and space to grow. Exactly what he wanted from her, he wasn't yet sure. But now that Paula Chamberlain had entered his life, he knew he couldn't let her go without putting up a fight.

Paula swam well; she'd already covered quite a distance. Cheating on his countdown, Quinn dived in after her, and his forceful crawl soon narrowed the space between them. With a deep intake of breath he dived and swam beneath her, surfacing right in her path.

"Gotcha!"

"Quinn...don't fool around," she spluttered, taken by surprise.

His triumphant grin faded. "Believe me, Paula, I'm not fooling. I'm determined to see you one way or another. Listen, the elephants have given me an idea. Come to the circus with me tonight. We can be sure that none of our people will be there."

"You're crazy."

"So I'm crazy. I'm also a nice guy to know. So try saying yes for a change. It's quite an easy word to get your tongue around."

Temptation was too strong to fight. "Okay, you win."

"That means yes?"

"That means yes."

Quinn grinned his pleasure. "Great. Where do I pick you up?"

"Nowhere. I'll meet you there. Say fifteen minutes before whatever time the show starts. Outside the entrance."

"I'll be waiting for you," Quinn said equably. Having won Paula's consent, he wasn't going to argue with her about this excessive caution. That could wait. He sensed that right now she wouldn't want to risk the chance of anyone they knew seeing them emerge from the water together. So, lifting a hand in goodbye, he struck out away from her, swimming parallel to the shoreline.

Paula trod water for a minute, watching him, until his head was no more than a distant blob. Then, with a sigh, she headed for the beach. Oh, God, what had she done? She was a fool to get involved with Quinn Barclay, but she couldn't help herself.

After another busy day at the Webberley villa—where, to Paula's relief, Quinn kept his distance—Lady Chamberlain held a meeting in the sitting room of her hotel suite. She called on each member of her team for an interim assessment of his or her own specialty. Paula went first.

"As far as the silverware goes," she reported enthusiastically, "this has to be the most important collection to hit the market in this decade. Ninety-five percent is of superb quality. And the ceramics are almost as good. Particularly the German porcelain. I don't think I've ever handled finer Meissen."

Lady C. gave a curt nod. "What about the paintings, Don?"

At first glance Don Heywood seemed an unlikely art expert. In his mid-thirties, he was tall and good-looking, with wheat-fair hair and a small mustache. He was keen on sports and kept in good shape playing cricket and squash. Ever since his wife, Judy, had given birth to twin girls five weeks earlier, he was apt to talk about them obsessively. In his work, though, Don was never given to rash statements. His expert opinion carried a lot of weight.

"A mixed bag," he said, choosing his words with care. "The Rembrandt and the Velasquez in the ballroom will both fetch record prices, no question, and there are several good Impressionists. I'm particularly hopeful about the Manets. Charles Webberley seems to have been specially keen on Flemish painters and he accumulated masses of stuff that's of no consequence. But—" Don gave a slow smile ''—I have a hunch that we'll be able to spring a couple of big surprises.''

''Such as?'' demanded Lady Chamberlain crisply.

''Well, I'll need to go deeper into this, of course. But there are two School of Rubens attributions that I'm inclined to think are largely the work of the master himself. A pair of new Rubens portraits would create a sensation. We could expect astronomical prices under the hammer.''

''That's very exciting, Don. Had we better go outside for another opinion?''

''Not for the moment, Lady C. Leave it with me for a while longer.''

This was the sort of situation Arabel delighted in. With luck it would put them a jump ahead of the opposition.

''Good work!'' She gave Don one of her most gracious smiles of approval. ''Now, Jeremy, what about the furniture? I noticed plenty of Hepplewhite at the villa.''

''There's plenty of a lot of sp-splendid things. Did you see the French gallery upstairs? What riches! There's the most gorgeous rococo drop-front *secrétaire* by D-Dubut that'll fetch a k-king's ransom.'' Jeremy Page was inclined to stutter when he was excited, a handicap that maddened him. Apart from this, he was invariably good-humored, always ready with a joke. He aimed at a Don Juan reputation, but never went far in putting it to the test. He adored food and was happily married to a woman who cooked superlatively. In the seven years Paula had known him, she'd watched his waistline steadily expanding. Now, approaching age forty, he was decidedly tubby.

Sidney Crowe was Chamberlain's most senior executive, and the financial brain. Only a couple of years older than Lady C., he looked a lot more than that. However, his shriveled features and stooped posture belied his forceful energy. Sidney fought back against arthritis with courage, and he was still a formidable figure on the auctioneer's rostrum, well respected and well liked. Sidney was an all-rounder, with an encyclopedic knowledge of every aspect of the art auction business. Since his wife's death seven years earlier, he had developed his special interest in the smaller objets d'art.

While giving his report to Lady Chamberlain, he sighed longingly over some Fabergé eggs. "A set of a dozen! How I covet them!"

"What will they fetch, Sidney?" she demanded.

He shrugged. "You'd better ask Paula that. She's the expert."

Lady C. looked impatient. She accepted deference to her own opinion, but to have it bandied about among others irritated her.

"All right, that's enough for now," she said. "All the signs are encouraging. It looks as if this sale will prove to be even more important than I dared hope. However, it isn't going to be plain sailing. Sylvester's is going all out to steal this from us. If nothing else, the fact that they've brought that wretched Barclay man over from New York is proof of it. Undoubtedly we can expect underhand tactics from him."

Paula couldn't let that go without a protest. Heedless of discretion, she burst out, "That's unfair. Quinn Barclay might have a reputation as a tough negotiator, but I've never heard anything to suggest that he doesn't play by the rules."

With careful deliberation Lady C. inserted a gold-tipped cigarette into her long holder. Don and Jeremy, on either side of her, each produced a lighter. Pausing a moment, she accepted a light from Jeremy.

"Perhaps, Paula, dear," she drawled, after taking a leisurely puff, "you and I have different standards by which we judge other members of our profession. It's a question of background."

Paula flushed at this gibe, but said forcefully, "It's not a question of background, it's a question of being unprejudiced. All I'm saying is..."

"Yes, dear?" inquired Lady C. silkily, pouncing on Paula's momentary hesitation. "Do give us the benefit of your thoughts."

There was a lot Paula could have said. But she feared it would emerge as a heated defense of Quinn. And Quinn Barclay was a man about whom she knew next to nothing. He might even be the rogue that Lady C. made him out to be. So Paula shrugged, feigning indifference.

Sidney Crowe remarked pacifically, "I take it we're all agreed that prestige is more important to us than profit in the case of the Webberley sale? As long as we don't come out of it with a trading loss, then..."

"That's obvious, Sidney," Lady Chamberlain said waspishly. "Handling the Webberley sale would establish the preeminence of Chamberlain's once and for all. We can't afford to lose it to Sylvester's." She inhaled through her long holder again, making the others wait until she chose to continue. "I'd dearly love to know the way their minds are working, but of course they will be operating a security as tight as our own."

The five of them shared thoughts on how best to present their proposals for the sale. It was necessary to convince the Webberley trustees that Chamberlain's would be able to command higher bids in the salesroom than their rival auction house, and to do so at a minimal commission.

"I'm inclined to the opinion," Arabel said weightily, "that New York would be the best venue for the sale of the paintings."

Don wasn't happy about that. "If we put forward New York as the most suitable venue to sell paintings, isn't it going to be a bit tricky? With a man like Quinn Barclay right on the spot, Sylvester's is in a dominant position."

Lady C. quelled him with a glance. "Don't be a defeatist, Don. Think positively. We are unquestionably the best. If we don't have faith in ourselves, no one else is going to."

Recluctantly Paula had to admire her mother-in-law. Arabel had many faults, but lack of courage wasn't one of them. Iain had inherited his mother's striking looks and her flair and instinctive feel for antiques. But not her courage.

At seven o'clock Lady Chamberlain decided to adjourn the meeting. "I have no dinner engagement for this evening," she announced in a queenly manner. "If any of you would care to join me in the Monaco Room at eight, you'd be welcome."

If the three men had other plans they kept quiet about them. Slightly thrown, Paula said quickly, "I think I'll skip dinner at the hotel this evening. I'd like to go for a walk and look around."

"As you wish, of course." Arabel had taken offense, though, and she let it show.

Paula turned to the door. "I'll see you in the morning, then."

"After your swim?"

"After my swim," Paula agreed blithely.

For her date with Quinn, Paula changed into slacks and a blue cotton sweater with a roll neckline. At seven-thirty she set out as if she were merely intent on a stroll. The circus was performing within walking distance of the hotel, starting at eight o'clock.

It wasn't until she was halfway there that Paula remembered about eating. Luckily there were plenty of cafés around. She dived into one to grab a sandwich and a cup of coffee. Walking on five minutes later, she found herself in a throng of people heading in the same direction. There were couples and family groups, with lots of excited children. The big top, a vast pink-and-white candy-striped tent, was pitched in a sports field close to the shore, surrounded by trucks and trailers and all the other paraphernalia of a traveling circus.

At first she couldn't see Quinn, and she was afraid that something might have prevented him from coming. Her sense of letdown made her realize just how much she'd been looking forward to this evening. Positioning herself near the entrance, she gazed around anxiously.

"Looking for someone, ma'am?" Quinn's voice came from right behind her. "Will I do?"

Paula whirled to face him, smiling her delight without pretense. Quinn laughed, but there was something more than just amusement in his expression. His deep blue eyes gave her a searching look.

"Want to know something, Paula? I was scared you weren't going to show."

"But I said I'd come."

"So you did. Maybe I'm not used to ladies who keep their word. Sorry if you couldn't find me, but I was buying tickets from the other pay booth. There wasn't such a long line at that one."

"Oh, I see."

His brows lifted. "Don't tell me you were worried?"

"Well..."

"I'm flattered. Come on, let's get inside before all the best seats are taken."

A mechanical organ was pumping out a lively march, and there was a cheerful buzz of conversation as they made their way into the big top. The smell of crushed grass and sawdust was strongly evocative, taking Paula back to her childhood. In such a jostling crowd it seemed only natural, sensible, for Quinn to take hold of her hand. But as his fingers closed around hers, Paula felt a thrill at the contact of his warm flesh. They edged their way along to a good position in the third row, and when they sat down Quinn still kept his fingers linked with hers. Paula made no attempt to pull her hand away. She felt happy in a way she hadn't known happiness in a long time.

"Fun, isn't it?" Quinn held out a bag of popcorn for her to dip into. "The one and only time I went to the circus before was on my tenth birthday. It was a special treat for me. We had fish and chips beforehand, I remember, and I was nearly sick with excitement."

"Was it just you and your parents? Or do you have brothers and sisters?"

"Just me and my mother. My father walked out on us when I was two and a half, leaving a heap of debts. Which meant that my mother spent the next few years trying to get her finances straightened out on the modest salary she earned as a bookkeeper. Treats like going to the circus didn't figure largely in my childhood."

"It must have been tough."

Quinn gave a slight shrug. "Maybe I missed out on some of the things most kids take for granted. But I'm not complaining. My mother was a very special lady."

"Was?"

"She died twenty years ago, when I was sixteen. But not before she'd seen to it that I went to a first-rate school. She was determined to give me a good start."

Paula smiled. "She'd have been proud of you, Quinn. Proud of the headway you've made in your career."

"I hope so, Paula. I hope so." He smiled back at her. "You haven't done so badly, either."

"But I started from a more privileged base, with my father already in the fine art business," Paula told him. Then a despondent thought struck her. Some of the privilege she hadn't been entitled to. A cloud hung over her past.

Quinn watched the shadows flit across Paula's lovely oval-shaped face. He wished he knew the reason for them, wished he could bring her comfort. But their relationship was too new and fragile for probing into secrets. Would it ever become anything deeper? he wondered. After this brief interlude in France, their paths would diverge. He'd be spending a week or maybe two in London, then he had to return to New York. An ocean would separate them. He pondered why this one woman should matter so much to him. Paula Chamberlain was something special.

The music wheezed to a stop, and there was an expectant hush. Then brassy fanfares. To a fresh burst from the organ, the horses entered, preening and prancing in their spangled harness. The show was off to a lively start.

Paula allowed herself to be swept along by the general mood of childlike enjoyment. She laughed out loud at the antics of the clowns, gasped in terror at the perilous feats of the trapeze artists. When one of the three elephants they'd seen in the sea plucked up the trainer in its trunk and seemed about to toss him into the audience, she clutched Quinn's arm in pretended alarm.

He smiled to himself, liking her spontaneity, the instinctive intimacy of the gesture. He knew that he and Paula were good news for each other. Her response to him this evening, away from Lady Chamberlain and the other people she worked with, was as natural and warm as he'd dared to hope.

Emerging after the show into a balmy evening, they turned their footsteps toward the sea. As they reached the promenade an appetizing aroma was wafting from a curbside stall.

"Let's try *le hot dog*...French style," Quinn suggested.

"Why not?" Suddenly Paula was ravenous. "Mustard with mine, please."

To go with the hot dogs, Quinn bought two plastic mugs of red wine drawn from a cask. They sat side by side on a stone wall facing the sea. The dark water was silvered by the rising moon.

"Mmm! This is good." Paula took a second large bite of the hot dog.

"It sure is!" Their shoulders and upper arms were touching, and Paula could sense the throb of his pulse. She drank some more of the wine and felt its glow in her veins.

"There's something I'm very curious about," Quinn said after a few moments' companionable silence.

"What's that?" she asked guardedly.

"Why did you decide to stay on at Chamberlain's after your husband's death?"

Paula frowned at his directness. "I was working there before I married Iain. That was how we met. Why shouldn't I have stayed on?"

"It's just that I know you were thinking of leaving."

"How in the world...?"

"You're forgetting that I'm one of Sylvester's directors. Lionel Fairhurst told me he'd talked to you about the possibility of your joining us."

"Oh!" This was something Paula hadn't anticipated. She said uneasily, "I was just considering my options. It was a question of judging what was best for my professional future.''

"That's why I'm surprised. You'd have had a lot more scope for your talents with Sylvester's.''

"Isn't that a matter of opinion?''

"No, Paula, it's a matter of fact.''

The balmy evening breeze seemed to have turned chill. She said stonily, "Are you trying to recruit me, Quinn? Is that the reason you've been pursuing me?''

"Absolutely not. I just want to get to know you. All the same, joining us might be worth another thought.''

This was a subject Paula didn't want to get into. She'd been a lot closer to joining Sylvester's after Iain's death than she was willing to admit to Quinn. In fact, her mind had been made up; it had seemed to be a sensible move. Since she and her mother-in-law had never pretended to like each other, Paula had reckoned that Arabel would be equally ready to sever their professional association. But it hadn't suited Lady Chamberlain to let her go, and she had powerful leverage. Paula had been shocked to discover that her mother-in-law knew the discreditable truth about her father. She'd confessed it to Iain when they were first married, feeling that it was wrong to keep such a dark secret from her husband. Stupidly—treacherously as it seemed to Paula—he had divulged this astonishing revelation to his mother. And Arabel had mentally filed away the information, to be used against Paula anytime it suited her.

With an inward shudder Paula recalled the scene. She had gone to see Lady C. in her sumptuous office at the Chamberlain headquarters in Mayfair to resign her job.

"I can't stop you from resigning, of course," Arabel had said with a chilling look. "However, if you're no longer a member of my organization, I shall no longer have reason to suppress the kind of illegal dealings your father indulged in. I shall follow the dictates of my conscience and let the truth emerge.''

''But that's monstrous. You can't mean it.''

''Oh, but I do, Paula. I've always regarded integrity in our profession to be of prime importance. One has a duty to show up those who betray it.''

''But my father's dead. What good could it possibly do anyone?''

''Nonetheless, a crime was committed. You should feel flattered, my dear, that I value your talent so highly that I'm willing to quiet my conscience for the sake of keeping you at Chamberlain's.''

Paula came back to the present with a start, realizing that Quinn had taken her hand. He stroked the fingers one by one.

''You were light-years away,'' he said in a tone of mild reproach. ''Hardly a compliment to me.''

''Sorry.'' She shook off her gloom and smiled at him.

''Better. You have the loveliest smile, Paula. It starts deep in your eyes and shines out and illumines your whole face. Are you going to tell me the reason for that dark frown a moment ago?''

She shrugged dismissively. ''A goose walked over my grave.''

''I can't believe it was so trivial,'' he said, his eyes serious. ''Not the way you were looking. Why don't you tell me about it? Maybe I can help.''

''Oh, leave it,'' she said testily.

''Take it easy. I'm not about to pry.'' He stood. ''How about going for a drive?''

''A drive?''

''My rental car is parked quite near. We could head along the coast for a few miles.''

"No, I don't think so," Paula said. "I should be getting back to the hotel."

"So early?"

"It's late enough. I agreed to go to the circus with you, that's all."

"It doesn't have to be all, Paula."

"Yes, it does." Her voice emerged as a little shrill.

Quinn read the warning. "Okay. But before we start back, what do we do tomorrow evening?"

"Nothing. We don't meet again."

His eyes on her face were keen, searching. "This can't be the end for us, Paula. It can't be. You know that."

She nodded her head slowly. Fate had crossed her path with Quinn's, and there was no way of avoiding a relationship growing between them. But she trembled at what it could mean for her.

"Quinn, you have to understand...it's really important to me that no one else should know about it, if we do agree to see each other."

"I don't see why."

"It's the way it has to be. I seriously mean that."

He was silent, and Paula could tell it went against the grain with him. But he finally accepted her terms with a nod. "For the time being. Come on, I'll drive you back to the hotel."

"No, thanks. I can walk."

Quinn cursed explosively, startling her. "Don't push me too far, Paula. Secret affairs aren't my style. I'll drive you back and drop you off at the corner near the hotel. Then you can walk in alone. Okay?"

She only hesitated a moment. "Okay."

The three or four minutes it took them to drive back along the tree-lined promenade passed in an uneasy silence. Glancing sideways, Paula could see the hostile set of

Quinn's features. She knew she had made him angry, and
she didn't know how to recapture a happy mood between
them. The sidewalks were thronged with couples, walking
with their arms entwined, unashamed of their interest in
each other. Why couldn't it be like that for her and Quinn?
she thought sadly.

He stopped the car a few yards short of the hotel's im-
posing entrance. "Here's where you get out."

Paula turned toward him. "Thank you for this evening, Quinn. I really enjoyed it."

"Did you?" He laughed and kept his eyes looking ahead
through the windshield. "I wish I could think that you
meant that, Paula, but it takes some believing."

"I'm sorry," she said unhappily. "I've tried to explain."

"Forget it," he snapped.

With a feeling of despondency, Paula turned away and
fumbled for the door catch.

"Paula..." he murmured.

She turned back expectantly. For a moment Quinn was
quite still, looking at her, then he lifted his hand to her
face. With the back of one finger he lightly caressed her
cheek.

"I'll see you in the morning, on the float," he said
softly.

Paula nodded her agreement, too choked up to trust her
voice.

Three

—

Paula awoke early to the sound of heavy rain beating against the windows and a gale-force wind. No swim this morning, that was obvious. She lay back on the pillows, staring at the ornate ceiling in a mood of deep depression. It was crazy, she tried telling herself, to be sunk in gloom just because she'd been robbed of a few minutes on the float with Quinn. A few minutes alone together in their private world.

The phone at her bedside tinkled melodiously. Lady C. with some change of plan? It could happen like that, any time of the day or night, whenever the whim entered her mother-in-law's mind.

Sighing, Paula lifted the phone. "Paula Chamberlain here."

"Hi!" It was Quinn's voice, and her spirits instantly lifted. "Shame about the rain, isn't it? Even if we didn't mind a wet swim, so to speak, the danger flags have been hoisted.''

"Who'd ever have expected this? I mean, after yesterday's marvelous weather.''

"Rain on the Riviera should be declared illegal,'' he agreed. "Our plans for the evening had better be under cover.''

"Right, but not too early. I have a very busy day scheduled. Lady C. is aiming to wrap things up here today, and we'll be returning to London tomorrow.''

"Same with my group. How about eight o'clock?''

"Better make it eight-thirty.''

"It's a deal,'' he said. "Did you sleep well?''

"Sure. I always do.''

"The advantage of an untroubled conscience.''

"How about yours, Quinn?''

"Driven snow doesn't come any purer than mine. Did you dream about me, Paula?''

"Certainly not.'' She snuggled back more comfortably against the pillows.

"What did you dream about, then? Or whom?''

She pretended to reflect a moment. "Well, I seem to remember this tall, incredibly attractive and intelligent man....''

"So it was me, after all.''

"Actually,'' she improvised, "he was a Frenchman.''

"Ah *oui*. I have—how you say it—a leetle bit of *le Français* in me from way back.''

Paula relented with a laugh. "Okay, *monsieur*, it must have been you.''

After a brief pause, Quinn said seriously, "Shall we have breakfast together someplace?''

He was back to pushing her, but Paula didn't want to make an issue of it. With a regretful sigh, loud enough for him to hear, she said, "Don't tempt me."

"You know what Oscar Wilde had to say on that subject?"

"Remind me."

"He said that the only way to get rid of a temptation is to yield to it."

"Then Mr. Wilde is about to be proved wrong."

Quinn groaned. "Women can be so heartless at times."

"No doubt you speak from vast experience."

"Oscar Wilde had something to say about experience, too."

"Which you're about to quote at me."

Quinn chuckled. "He said that experience is the name we give to our mistakes."

"Your love affairs can't all have been mistakes, surely?"

"Oh, Paula! What countless numbers you imply. Did you never make mistakes?"

"I did not."

"I find that hard to believe. Weren't there at least one or two men you swooned over as a teenager that you shudder to think about now?"

"Oh, well...if you're talking about that sort of thing."

Quinn's tone became caressingly soft. "I'll tell you something, Paula...if I'd met you back then, I'd have instantly fallen head over heels in love with you."

She longed to ask what about *now*? But she suspected that Quinn had laid that very trap for her. Instead she remarked airily, "You must have been remarkably unbalanced in those days."

"On the contrary, I was remarkably mature."

"So how come you made all those mistakes?"

Quinn's laugh came loudly over the phone. "Got me there. You're just too smart for me at this hour of the morning. We'll resume this conversation over dinner. Eight-thirty, right? I'll be waiting at the same spot where I dropped you off last night."

Paula pondered long and hard over *The Five Senses*, a delightful set of painted porcelain figures each about eight inches high, that had all the hallmarks of authentic early Meissenware. Yet she was uneasy about them. Intuition more than knowledge was sending out all kinds of warning signals. Were they genuine, or extremely clever fakes? In the end, to resolve the matter, she went along to the secretary's office on the second floor, where records were kept of every work of art in the Webberley collection.

Finding the entry on the computer, she was almost relieved to see that Charles Webberley hadn't been taken for a ride. He had bought the set of figures—at a good but fair price—as the work of a talented Victorian forger.

While she was still jotting down some notes, Don Heywood walked in. Rather pleased with herself, Paula told him about her discovery.

"Clever girl!" he said admiringly. "Mind you, I'm finding quite a bit of fakery here in my own line. But, genuine or not, almost every piece is interesting in its own right. Old man Webberley knew what he liked."

On a similar errand to Paula's, Don tapped into the computer. They were both engrossed when Lady C. looked around the door.

"Ah, you two! I wanted to let you know that I shan't be returning to London with the rest of you tomorrow." She paused, and Don asked the invited question. "Why is that, Lady C.?"

"I've had an invitation to spend the weekend with a cousin of mine at Monte Carlo." As a casual throwaway, Arabel added, "That's the Princess Naomi d'Arcadina, you know. Dear Naomi was so pressing that I felt obliged to accept."

"How nice for you," Don murmured. "I expect she has a beautiful place?"

"Indeed it is. A charming *fin de siècle* villa. And barely a stone's throw from the Royal Palace."

Don's raised eyebrows shared a joke with Paula. In tiny Monte Carlo, it would be difficult for anything to be more than a stone's throw from the Royal Palace. He said pleasantly, "I was just about to get some coffee. May I bring you a cup, Lady C.?"

"No, I'll come downstairs with you, Don. Will you join us, Paula?"

"I might as well. I'm finished here for the time being."

As they descended the stairs, Paula gave Don a lead into his favorite subject. "All well at home? How are the twins doing?"

"Oh, Paula, they really are a fantastic pair. Judy told me on the phone last night that she had them weighed yesterday, and they've each gained more than a half pound in the past week." His hand went to his coat pocket. "Did I show you the photos I took the day they came home from the hospital?"

"Really, Don," Lady C. rebuked. "You mustn't become a bore about those babies of yours."

He flushed a deep crimson, and Paula felt guilty about laying him open to this. "I'm not sure that I've seen all the pictures, Don," she said quickly, untruthfully. "You must show them to me later."

They had reached the small room where refreshments were available throughout the day. Don hurried forward to open the door and stood aside for the two women to enter. A hum of voices came from inside; the entire Sylvester's team was assembled there. Lady Chamberlain's lips tightened in vexation, but she marched in with her head thrown back. Paula's glance flew to Quinn, standing taller than the other men. He acknowledged her with a flicker of his eyes as he nodded a polite greeting to the newcomers.

Lionel Fairhurst came forward, a cup of coffee in his hand. "Good morning, Lady C. Let's hope this rain soon clears up. Not quite what one expects down here in the South of France."

"I suppose not," Arabel observed coolly. "But the state of the weather is hardly relevant when there's a job to be done."

Quinn had moved around the buffet table, and he stood beside Paula as she poured herself a cup of coffee from the urn.

"You must have been deprived of your swim this morning, Mrs. Chamberlain," he remarked in a conversational tone.

"My swim?" What was Quinn up to?

"I seem to recall your mentioning that you like to swim in the mornings. So do I, sometimes. If this weather improves, I'll look out for you tomorrow."

Paula tried to angle a frown that only Quinn would see. "I doubt if I'll have time for a swim tomorrow," she said in a cool voice.

"Pity. It'll be your last opportunity."

Paula took her cup to the window and stood gazing out at the rain that was still pouring down in torrents. Quinn, darn him, followed her and spoke quietly from behind her shoulder.

"Paula, why are you so on edge?"

"As if you didn't know," she muttered, without turning around.

"Because I mentioned your morning swims? What's in that to make you mad?"

"You wouldn't care, of course," she said bitterly, "if it all came out about us."

"There isn't a lot to come out," he observed in a dry tone.

"Paula!" Lady C.'s voice rang out from across the room. Paula swung around to find that her mother-in-law was glaring at them with disapproval.

"Yes, Lady C.?"

"Please come over here. I wish to speak to you."

"My God, what a virago she is," Quinn said, amused. "It astonishes me you tolerate her."

Paula didn't reply. She crossed, but unhurriedly, to where her mother-in-law stood delicately nibbling a buttered scone.

"What is it?" Paula inquired.

"You should know better than to let that man inveigle you into conversation."

"Inveigle?" Paula poured scorn into her voice. "It was just polite chitchat."

"Don't you believe it. His type has a motive for everything he does. Most probably he was chatting you up with the deliberate intention of annoying me."

"If you really think that, Lady C., wouldn't your best counterploy be to appear not to have noticed?"

"I have no intention of letting you make a fool of yourself. Quinn Barclay is a dangerous man. I wonder that even Sylvester's finds it worth employing someone like him. He has no breeding. I suppose you know that? He came from nothing."

"I'd have said that makes it all the more commendable that he's reached his present level, on the board of Sylvester's."

A sharp intake of breath sounded between Lady C.'s lips. "Are you being willfully obtuse, Paula? But then, your own background leaves a lot to be desired."

This was yet another reminder, Paula thought furiously, of the gun her mother-in-law held to her head. She was saved the need to find a suitable response by an interruption from Lionel Fairhurst.

"My dear Lady C.," he said, approaching her again with a beaming smile. "The thought has just occurred to me that as this will be our last evening here, should we not mark the occasion by all having dinner together? Now what do you say to that?"

Paula was swept by dismay. Her precious evening with Quinn was to be snatched away from her. By an ironic twist, it was Arabel's indomitable hostility that came to her rescue. Fixing Lionel Fairhurst with a withering gaze, she stated, "I think it would be most inappropriate. This is not a social gathering, Mr. Fairhurst."

"But we are not enemies, Lady Chamberlain. Rivals, yes . . . and may the better of us win."

"We will, Mr. Fairhurst. You may be sure of it."

He chuckled. "Well, well, I'll let you cling to your illusions while you can."

She regarded him with haughty challenge. "I wonder if you'll repeat your dinner invitation in a few weeks' time, when the Webberley trustees have announced their decision about the sale."

"A nice thought. The winner entertaining the loser."

"We shall see, Mr. Fairhurst. We shall see."

From across the room, Paula caught Quinn's eye. He looked greatly amused at the exchange. She felt only a sweeping sense of relief that her evening with Quinn was safe.

By eight-thirty, when she and Quinn set out in his rental car, the rain had stopped. A tenuous mist hung in the air, turned to a golden gauze by the lowering sun. Quinn drove a dozen miles along the coast to an ancient walled town. For a while they sat on the quayside, their backs to the cluster of red-roofed houses that had been built in terraces up the steep hillside. In the small harbor before them, the fishing boats jostled one another at their moorings, awaiting their dawn departure.

Paula had already tackled Quinn in the car about the episode that morning at the Webberley villa.

"What in the hell got into you?" she'd demanded. "You must have known that I wouldn't like it, the way you were talking to me."

"Sorry." He shrugged. "It just seemed a good opportunity to let other people see the two of us getting better acquainted."

"I thought I'd made it clear that I don't want anyone to link us together, Quinn. Not at all."

"Dammit to hell," he said, and was mutinously silent as he edged the car past a donkey cart on the narrow, twisting coastal road. "I can't pretend to understand," he went on in a softer tone, "but if that's the way it has to be, then okay. In public, Paula Chamberlain and Quinn Barclay are just slight business acquaintances."

Now, their spat behind them, Paula still couldn't shake off her mood of sadness. It seemed accentuated by a wistful quality of the soft evening light.

"I know the feeling," said Quinn, breaking the silence.

Startled by his apparent insight, she reacted with irony. "Into mind reading now, are we?"

He ignored the gibe. "It's common to experience a sort of melancholy in places that are steeped in history."

Her own melancholy was more about the future than the past, Paula reflected. But that wasn't something to discuss with Quinn right now, so she picked up his cue. "All these Roman relics in Provence do give the place a special aura."

"Not just *relics*. Did you know that some of the public water supply is carried by aqueducts built in Roman times? The local people have a strong sense of history in them. All the recent tourist development is just something laid over the surface. The basic pattern of life hasn't changed all that much." Quinn gestured to where a black-garbed woman sat placidly mending a fishing net farther along the quay. "If we'd been sitting here three, four, five hundred years ago, we'd probably have seen much the same sight."

Paula gave him a sideways glance, surprised. "I'd have thought you were a man who always looked ahead, not back to the past."

"So I'm indulging myself for once." He stood and took her hand. "Come on, let's go find someplace to eat."

They didn't need to look far. Right on the waterfront was a pretty bistro, Chez Félix, with a lush fig tree growing up the wall. Inside, under a stone-vaulted ceiling, the tables were spread with red checkered cloths. The white-aproned patron led them to a position by a window. With a flourish, he struck a match and lit a candle that was thrust into the neck of a bottle.

"*Apéritifs, mes amis?*"

"White wine for me," said Paula.

"The local wines around here are red," Quinn told her. "Would you like to try some?"

"Oh, yes. Red, then."

In a moment the patron was back bearing a dark green bottle. The cork was extracted with ceremony, a little wine poured for Quinn's approval. The man stood back, a hand resting on his paunch. "Good, is it not so? A fine wine. Ah, *oui!*"

It was good. Very good. Dark ruby red, full-bodied and potent. Yet smooth as silk on the palate.

"The food's good here, too," Quinn commented, studying the menu card that had been presented to them with pride.

"Have you been here before, then?" Paula queried.

"Uh-huh."

"When was that?"

"Oh . . . sometime last autumn. I came this way to evaluate a collection of watercolors that Sylvester's was handling."

"Oh, I see. Business." Relieved, Paula lifted her own menu and perused it.

"I didn't come *here* on business, though," Quinn informed her. "I seem to remember we ate *loup de mer au fenouil*. That's sea perch with fennel. Delicious."

"We?" She hadn't meant to ask; it just came out.

His blue eyes regarded her blandly across the top of the menu. "Me and the lady I was with."

For Paula, Chez Félix had lost its charm. One thing was for sure, she wasn't about to choose sea perch with fennel. Perhaps the lamb. She glanced up to ask Quinn a carefully casual question and found him grinning at her.

"What's funny?"

"I was teasing you, Paula."

"Teasing?"

"The lady I brought here was a *grande dame* of around seventy-five. Madame Frenais is the great-aunt of the guy I play squash with in New York, and I'd promised to look her up and take her out to dinner. She named this place as serving the best food in town."

"How gallant!" Paula lifted her shoulders in an elaborate shrug. "Am I supposed to care how many ladies you might have brought here before, old or young?"

"Don't you care?" Quinn's eyes were serious now, asking several questions all at once.

"Well..." Another shrug. "A tiny bit, I suppose."

"More than a tiny bit?" he cajoled.

"All right, then," she conceded. "More than a tiny bit."

"You're jealous."

"I'm jealous."

"Good. That's how I want it to be." Quinn touched her hand where it lay on the table, lightly drawing his fingers down the back of hers. "Just as I'm jealous of all the other men you've known. Tell me about your husband, Paula. Was it a good marriage? Were you happy together?"

"Of course," she said quickly.

"I want a better answer than that. You and Iain were together for... how many years? Five?"

"Nearer six."

"That's plenty of time for cracks to start showing. Did they, Paula?"

"That's a very personal question."

"I feel personal where you're concerned. I want to know all about you. Would your marriage have lasted if your husband hadn't died?"

"I hope so. I like to think so."

"But you don't sound very certain."

"I guess every marriage has its ups and downs. We had a few problems along the way, but... I think we could have worked them out." Paula was annoyed with herself for having admitted more than she'd intended. She became brisk. "Can we please change the subject?"

Quinn nodded slowly. "For now, anyhow."

The waiter approached their table, wanting to know if they were ready to order. Relieved, Paula applied herself again to the menu.

"It's so difficult to choose from all these tempting dishes," she murmured, her thoughts still elsewhere.

"The sea perch comes with my personal recommendation," Quinn reminded her helpfully.

"So I'll try the sea perch." She sat back, grinning at him. "If it was good enough for a *grande dame*, it'll be good enough for me."

For appetizers they chose duck pâté, and the meal progressed at a leisurely pace. They talked easily about nothing of importance, just enjoying each other's company. The candles on the tables seemed to burn more brightly as the daylight faded.

Paula was spooning a delicious *crème caramel* when Quinn said, "Tell me some more about yourself."

"You know quite enough already."

He shook his head. "Not nearly enough. I know almost nothing about you before you were married, beyond the fact that you were Ralph Grayling's daughter. Tell me about your childhood."

"There's not a lot to say about it. Except that my mother died when I was nine. Then it was just Dad and me."

"So you, too, were raised by just one parent. That's something we have in common."

She'd had the same thing in common with Iain, whose father had died when he was fourteen. But whereas her father had taught her to be independent, and whereas it seemed that Quinn's mother had done likewise for him, Arabel Chamberlain had raised her son almost as a puppet on strings.

"I wish I'd met your father," Quinn went on. "Somehow I never did. Ralph Grayling had a reputation as one of the most knowledgeable dealers around, especially when it came to the Impressionists."

Paula felt a chill of alarm. She studied Quinn's face thoughtfully. Was he probing her for more than he pretended? Did he somehow have an inkling that her father had once lapsed from his habitual straight path?

"Tell me more about *you*," she said, to get off the subject. "What sparked your interest in this profession?"

"I guess I always wanted to be involved in art. In my boyhood fantasies I saw myself as a world-famous painter. But it was hammered into me by my mother that an ability to draw and paint wasn't going to pay the rent unless I was exceptionally lucky. My degree at the university was in art history. Just when I was wondering how best to capitalize on this, Sylvester's had a vacancy for a trainee in the department of modern art, which was my special interest at the time. I applied and got the job."

"Then raced to the top of the ladder."

His eyes were serious. "The top? I have a long way to go yet, Paula."

"No limits to your ambition?"

"A limited ambition is a contradiction in terms. Take yourself. Can you imagine reaching a level where you'll sit back and feel that you've achieved it all?"

Paula thought about that. "Professional achievement isn't the only thing in life, Quinn."

"That could be true." Then, as if it followed logically, he said, "Go on telling me about you and Iain. Why did you marry him?"

"Are you hinting," she flared, "that it was because Iain was in line to inherit Chamberlain's?"

"Take it easy, Paula. I'm hinting nothing. I'm just asking."

"We fell in love. That's the usual reason for getting married, isn't it?"

"It should be. And how long did the loving last?"

"What is this, an inquisition?"

"Sorry." Quinn smiled contritely. "I just want to know what I'm up against. I find it difficult to picture you and Iain Chamberlain tethered in wedded bliss."

"I don't know why you should say that," Paula protested. But she did know. Quinn was too perceptive in guessing the problems she'd faced. She had been wildly in love with Iain at first; and even later, love had still remained. His death had been a great sorrow to her. But their marriage had been blighted right from the start by his mother's constant interference.

"Iain Chamberlain wasn't renowned for his strength of character," Quinn said quietly. "Rumor has it that he was completely under his mother's thumb."

Paula shifted uncomfortably in her seat. "Lady C. is a very domineering person. Everyone knows that."

"She tries to be." A faint smile touched his lips. "I can't somehow see *you* kowtowing . . . either as her daughter-in-law or as her employee. Am I wrong?"

In the minor, everyday differences of opinion, Paula could claim that she stood up to Arabel Chamberlain. But in the larger battle of wills it was a different story. She said carefully, "She and I understand each other. And respect each other."

"Respect isn't what I've seen in your eyes when I've watched you with Lady C."

"Oh? I didn't know you'd been spying on me."

Quinn laughed. "Well, you know now. And you can't provoke me by using a dirty word like spying. I observe you, Paula, because I'm extremely interested in you."

"Well, I wish you wouldn't be."

"Do you?" His voice was soft and low. "Do you really?"

Paula fingered her wineglass without lifting it. "It'll all be academic, anyway, after tomorrow," she said, the reminder bringing a chilling shadow.

"Wrong," he said. "I'll be spending a while in London before returning to New York. A week at least."

A rush of emotion tore Paula two ways. "That's wonderful, Quinn," she said. But her mind was filled with dismay at the problems she saw looming.

"It would be even more wonderful if I could persuade you to stay on here through the weekend."

"Stay on?" she gasped.

"Until Sunday, I thought."

"It's a nice idea," she said unsteadily, "but I don't see how I can."

"Why? Have you something lined up in London that can't be put off?"

"No, it's not that. But . . . what reason would I give for not returning with the others?"

"The fiery dragon lady won't be here. She's off to hobnob with her titled relative in Monte Carlo, as she's made sure everybody knows. So you don't have to worry about her bothering you. As for the others, just tell them you've decided to give yourself a minivacation."

Crosscurrents of thought raced through Paula's mind. Quinn was right; there was no valid reason that she shouldn't stay over until Sunday. There wasn't a single person, now that Iain was dead, who had any sort of right to question what she did on her own time. The idea was incredibly tempting. If she did stay over, though, her relationship with Quinn would take a big leap forward. The way he was looking at her, the way she felt about him, there'd be a commitment between them. Did she want that? Was she ready for a new relationship? With *any* man, let alone this particular man who brought a package of problems with him?

"I . . . I don't know," she said uncertainly.

"Please!" Quinn put a lot of emotion into that one quiet word.

Still Paula hesitated. Then quite suddenly her dilemma dissolved. The answer was simple, obvious. She'd be crazy not to stay over. Whatever the future might hold, she'd never regret this weekend with Quinn as much as she'd regret having passed up the opportunity.

"Okay, I'll stay."

"Wonderful!" Quinn picked up her hand and bent his head to kiss it. His lips were warm and tender, sensuously exciting. "We'll check with the hotel as soon as we get back about extending our stay. If there's a problem, we can always find another hotel."

"Yes." They were conspirators, making plans.

"Tomorrow," Quinn suggested, "we'll rent a boat and explore the Îles d'Hyères."

Paula had seen the chain of low islands lying several miles offshore, green-and-purple shadowed. Curiously remote. A beckoning haven for two people who just wanted to be alone in each other's company.

"Have you been to the islands before?" she asked.

"No, it'll be the first time."

That made it perfect. Together they would explore new territory. It would belong to them and only them . . . Paula and Quinn.

Four

At about eight o'clock next morning the phone rang in Paula's room. It was Quinn.

"Did I wake you?"

"Of course not! I've been up for nearly an hour." Paula omitted explaining that she'd been too restless to remain in bed and had been prowling around her room aimlessly. It was a beautiful morning and she'd have loved to swim. But after stating publicly that she'd be too busy, she was forced to deny herself that pleasure.

"We have to make plans, Paula. Did you call the desk about keeping your room for an extra day?"

"Yes. They said okay."

"Same here. I also called the airport to check there'd be seats available on tomorrow evening's flight. I'm just back from a walk to the harbor. I've rented a powerboat for the day."

"You've been busy."

"So what time do we meet?"

"Well, the others will all have left the hotel by eleven o'clock, so as soon as you like after that." She knew that Quinn would be impatient with this cautious attitude on her part, but that was just too bad. She wasn't about to take unnecessary risks. She had it all figured out in her mind. A car was coming to take Arabel to Monte Carlo at ten-thirty. After that, Paula decided, would be the right time to announce that she'd decided to stay for an extra day.

Shortly before ten-thirty, Paula went down and found Arabel sitting with Sidney and Jeremy in the lobby coffee shop.

"Ah, Paula, I wondered if you'd manage to put in an appearance before I left."

Paula ignored the implied criticism and smiled amicably. "It looks as if you'll have lovely weather for your weekend. Quite a change after yesterday."

"What are your plans for tomorrow, Arabel?" asked Sidney in his usual self-appointed role of keeping things sweet. "Have you decided which flight you'll be taking back to London?"

"Not yet, Sidney. There are several to choose from, I understand. Now, when you settle up at the desk, do make sure they haven't overcharged us for telephone calls. Hotels are notoriously careless about such things. Ah, I see that my chauffeur has arrived."

The moment Lady Chamberlain had departed, with a flurry of last-minute instructions, they all relaxed.

"I still have to finish my packing," Sidney said. "Arabel wanted to go through some figures with me, and it's put me all behind." He consulted his watch. "Shall I meet you down here in fifteen minutes?"

"As a matter of fact . . ." Paula began.

Already turning away, Sidney and Jeremy glanced back at her questioningly.

"As a matter of fact, I won't be returning with you. I thought I'd take advantage of this glorious weather and stay on until tomorrow."

"Hey, that's an idea," said Jeremy. "Want me to join you?"

"Who're you kidding? I bet you can't wait to get home to Myra's cooking." To escape the need for any further conversation in the elevator, she lied. "I have to go see about the change in my flight reservation. See you Monday, back at the office."

There, it was done. So easy in the eventuality. A half hour later, the men having left for the airport, Paula set out from the hotel to meet Quinn.

Quinn watched her approaching along the crowded sidewalk, unaware of him as yet. There was sheer beauty in the way she walked, in the fluid grace of her slender body and the easy swing of her long legs. He didn't attempt to compare Paula with other women; she was in a class all her own. This morning she wore her hair down, and the sheening dark strands floated out behind her, tossed by the breeze. She looked incredibly sexy, incredibly wonderful. He knew now that in his meeting Paula Chamberlain his life had reached a turning point. Where did he go from here? Finding the answer to that question had top priority in his mind.

When Paula spotted him, while still fifteen yards away, her face lit up in a smile that made Quinn's heart skip a beat.

"Hi, lovely lady!" he called. Paula ran forward to him; then, suddenly hit by shyness, she stopped short of going into his arms.

"Hi to you."

"I searched around for a boat that was named for you, Paula. See!" Quinn gestured to where a sleek powerboat was tied up at the foot of some steps.

Paula read the name painted on its prow. *La Belle Dame*. She gave Quinn a quiet smile, still feeling a little nervous. This was the man with whom she was about to embark on an affair. Up until a few days ago she hadn't even met him, yet now he rated as the most important person in her life. Was she a total idiot to let her heart take over from her head?

"Ready to go?" he asked.

"Sure am."

As she started to descend the worn steps, Quinn gripped her elbow. There was a sweet intimacy in the pressure of his fingers that was wonderfully reassuring. He must have sensed how she was feeling, she thought gratefully. She turned her head to give him a quick smile. In that instant, as their eyes fused, there was complete togetherness. Quinn leaned toward her, and they kissed.

At the foot of the steps he held the boat steady while Paula stepped down into the cockpit, then leaped aboard himself. Casting off the line, he started the engine. He carefully nosed a path between the other moored boats. Once clear, he opened the throttle and, with a muted roar, they skimmed the sunlit sea.

"Your people get away okay?" he inquired.

Paula nodded.

"Mine won't be leaving until after lunch," he said.

She nodded again, without comment. Quinn slanted her a questioning look. "Did you know that they wouldn't all be leaving by the same plane?"

"Oh, yes, I knew. Otherwise..."

"Otherwise, what?"

She shrugged, not replying, and Quinn could read her mind. So she was still taking a cautious attitude about their relationship, which was damned stupid and totally unjustified. He wanted to make an issue out of it, but some instinct warned him that this would be a tactical error. Right now, at the start of their weekend, Paula was in a fragile mood. He could understand that. But although he let it go, Quinn seethed inwardly. A tiny cloud had appeared to spoil the perfection of their time together.

They tied up at the quayside of a diminutive harbor. After the noisy bustle of the mainland coast, the island was a haven of tranquillity. A tiny village of stone houses was guarded by a small, crenellated fortress. At the one and only inn they drank wine in the cool shade of a juniper tree, and asked for a bottle to take out. The friendly patron was happy to provide them with crusty sandwiches filled with cheese and roast meat. He found a plastic tote bag for them to carry their picnic.

An hour's climbing brought them to the heights. The village below seemed miles away; the sapphire sea lay all around, sparkling in the noonday sunshine. They were quite alone. Since leaving the inn they hadn't even seen anyone else.

"How about some more wine?" Quinn suggested. "That climb has made me thirsty."

"Good idea."

Crouching, he opened the tote bag he'd carried on his shoulder.

"Damn!"

"Why damn?"

"I remembered a corkscrew, but I forgot to ask for glasses or mugs or whatever."

"What's wrong with drinking out of the bottle?"

"Tastes better that way," he agreed, as he drew the cork.

Paula accepted the bottle from him and took a swig. A trickle of the red wine ran down her chin, and Quinn wiped it away with the tip of his forefinger. It was a little gesture that somehow seemed incredibly intimate. Handing the bottle back to him, she sat down on the springy turf with her legs curled up. A smell of crushed wild thyme was released and floated on the warm breeze.

"Let's see what's to eat," she said.

While they ate their lunch, their appetites sharpened by the open air, they started to talk about the Webberley collection.

"I don't believe I've ever seen so much silver in one place before," Paula said. "But some of it really surprised me."

"Fakes, you mean?"

"Not only the odd fake, but there are pieces that wouldn't fetch much on a street stall. I heard somewhere that Charles Webberley was a man who collected more for his own pleasure than with an eye to investment."

"That certainly goes for the paintings. There's a treasure hoard at that villa, but also some charming rubbish. Even so, I expect the glamour attaching itself to the sale will make buyers bid far more than it's worth."

"You think so? Aren't people in New York too astute for that?"

Quinn shot her an amused look. "Is New York where Chamberlain's would hold the paintings auction?"

"No comment." Improvising quickly, she went on, "I was taking it for granted that Sylvester's would think in terms of New York, having the brilliant Quinn Barclay right there on the spot to handle it for them."

"So that's what you meant! I wonder what gave me the idea you were fishing?"

Paula grinned at him playfully. "You can't blame a girl for trying."

"You should have waited for the wine to have taken more effect."

"On you? Or on me?"

Quinn threw back his head and laughed. "I think we'd better make a pact, don't you? No shop talk."

"Suits me."

He sobered and gave her a long, searching look that seemed to melt her bones. "Me, too, Paula. I vote we forget all about Chamberlain's and Sylvester's and the Webberley collection. Let's just concentrate on you and me."

When they'd eaten all they wanted, they put what was left of the food into the tote bag and strolled on. Birds sang around them on the sunny hillside, and there was a wonderful scent of wildflowers. Quinn held her hand, linking his fingers with hers. Paula was thankful that he hadn't tried to force the pace of their intimacy. Just this much physical contact was making her pulses pound and her head swirl.

The rugged hillside, with its short, blossom-studded turf, gradually gave way to pine woods. Lances of sunlight, striking through the foliage, made patterns of light and shade at their feet.

Presently Quinn halted and drew Paula around to face him. For long, heady moments they gazed at each other, and she felt a honeyed sweetness flood her body. When Quinn drew her against him, she slid her arms about his waist and released a deep sigh.

"Why the sigh?" he murmured.

"Because I'm feeling happy."

"Strange logic!" His hands roved her back, sliding down the ridges of her spine. "Does that mean you smile when you're feeling sad?"

"Sometimes."

"Problem. How do I read you when you smile at me?"

"You'll just have to wonder." Paula lifted her face so she could touch her lips to the tip of his nose. "When I was a small girl I used to burst into floods of tears when something specially nice happened."

"Not anymore?"

"Well . . . not lately."

"Pity! It would have given me the chance to kiss your tears away."

"Like in the elevator?"

"Not like that. Like this . . ." Quinn softly pressed his lips to each of her eyes in turn, lingering caressingly. Then his mouth skimmed across her cheek, searching out every curve and hollow, tasting the silken texture of her skin. The tip of his tongue probed her ear until Paula shivered with the exquisite sensation.

"I suppose," he whispered, "in your contrary way you're shivering because you're warm?"

"Something like that." Her voice was husky with emotion.

Standing close like this she could feel Quinn's body trembling, feel the betraying stir of his desire. His breath was warm on her face. Slowly he brought his mouth to hers, his lips moving against it softly and sensuously. After an instant of nervous hesitation, Paula welcomed the kiss warmly, allowing her lips to melt and part to receive the exciting gift of his tongue. She felt a lovely warm pulsation suffusing her limbs, and every nerve cell tingled with excitement. Then desire hit her, erupting through her whole body in a hot, fluid rush. She clung hard to Quinn and they kissed with a wild, hungry passion, only breaking apart when they were both breathless.

Paula glanced away, unable to meet his eyes. Quinn stroked her cheekbone with the back of one finger.

"I knew it would be like this for us, Paula. I sensed it from the very moment we met."

She swallowed, finding it strangely difficult to formulate words. "Since Iain...there hasn't been anyone. What happened just now...it took me by surprise."

"Darling, I understand. You don't have a thing to worry about." Quinn put his fingers under her chin and turned her face toward him. "I'm not going to rush you. We'll take things one step at a time." He smiled wryly. "I guess it would be a good idea for us to walk on, yes?"

Paula was only half aware of their surroundings as they descended the hillside back to the island's harbor, where their rented boat rocked gently at its mooring. The sun, beginning its westward descent, glittered dazzlingly on the sea. A white goat was tethered to a scrubby tree, and it watched them with mild interest as they walked past.

"There are other islands to explore, if you'd like to move on," said Quinn.

She shook her head. "I love it here."

"So do I, Paula." His eyes were warm with tenderness.

They stopped by the inn again for another glass of wine; a white wine this time with a pale greenish tinge. It was beautifully cool and refreshing, but also rather heady.

"I believe you're trying to make me tipsy, Quinn," she accused.

"Aren't you a bit tipsy already? I am...from the sun and the soft air and the quiet sense of peace. And from you! From you most of all."

Paula said nothing, but she met his eyes in a smiling glance. She felt extraordinarily happy, her doubts and fears laid aside. Just looking at Quinn made her feel weak and breathless. She loved to watch the play of light on the angled features of his face, loved to watch his unconscious gestures. He used his hands a lot while he was talking, sometimes as a prop for his chin, sometimes rubbing his forehead, sometimes pointing, sometimes with his fingers spread wide for emphasis. And his voice was sheer heaven to listen to, a dark rich baritone that curled its way into her very bloodstream. Paula knew by now that she was in love with him; how much she loved him it scared her to think about.

A ginger cat that had been dozing in the sunlit doorway roused itself and jumped up into Paula's lap, demanding attention. She fondled the silky fur of its throat, and it stretched its head back and purred ecstatically. The patron came bustling out to remove the cat, full of apologies.

"No, let it stay," said Paula. "It's beautiful."

"Could we have dinner here this evening?" Quinn inquired.

"But assuredly, *monsieur*. If we know you are coming, my wife will prepare a fine meal for you."

Quinn glanced at Paula. "Shall we say about eight o'clock?"

She nodded happily.

They left the inn and walked again, holding hands. This time they chose a path that hugged the rocky shore. Quinn laid his arm across her shoulders and drew her against his side. With her arm wrapped around his waist, she felt a wonderful sense of closeness between them. As if they were already lovers. Which, soon now, they would be. The thought of it sent excitement spiraling through her, and she quivered with joyous anticipation. But there was no urgency for her; that was the beauty of this day away from the real world. She and Quinn had time to savor every moment of their coming together. For the present, just to be with him, sometimes talking, sometimes silent, was all the joy she could handle.

They had half circled the island when they came to a tiny cove sheltered by low cliffs. To reach it they had to scramble down a boulder-strewn slope, and then they were on soft golden sand that yielded underfoot. Seabirds circled and swooped above them, uttering their evocative cries, but otherwise there was only the whisper of breaking wavelets.

Turning to face her, Quinn lightly caressed her shoulders, letting his fingers slip beneath the dark mane of her hair. Then he dipped his head to kiss her on the mouth. It was a kiss that started quietly, making no demands, but Paula was eager to respond as throbs of excitement pulsed through her veins. Parting her lips, she let the tip of her tongue touch his, reveling in the sweet intimacy as they explored and tasted.

Seconds flowed into minutes. When at long last the kiss ended, Quinn said, "Let's swim, darling."

"But . . . our things are in the boat."

"Does that matter? There's nobody around to see us." She still hesitated, and he added coaxingly, "I want to undress you. I want to look at you."

Paula felt too knotted with emotion to speak. She wanted this, too—she hadn't any doubts about it. But now the moment was here she felt painfully nervous and embarrassed.

"Yes?" he pressed, his voice a vibrant whisper in his throat.

She nodded silently. Quinn kissed her mouth again, softly, tenderly, then drew back to undo the buttons of her yellow cotton shirt. One by one he eased them through their buttonholes, then finally he slipped the shirt off her shoulders so that it fell to the sand. His hands were shaking now, his fingers less deft as he searched for the fastening of her bra and drew away the lacy garment.

"You have such beautiful breasts," he said in a wondering tone, his eyes drinking in her loveliness. His hands came up slowly and reverently to cup their soft weight, and Paula trembled at the almost unbearable pleasure of his touch.

Quinn kissed her again, his mouth trailing around the curve of her jawbone, skimming down the soft flesh of her throat to the cleft between her breasts. Here he lingered, burying his face in her warm, scented flesh. Then, sinking to his knees, he unclipped the waistband of her slacks and drew down the zipper. Moments later Paula was naked, and he gazed upon her with eyes that glowed in awed appreciation.

"You're exquisite," he breathed. "Perfect."

Paula was intensely moved. Iain had never treated her with this tender reverence. His lovemaking had always been a swift tumult of passion.

Standing again, Quinn quickly threw off his own clothes until he, too, was naked. Paula looked at him admiringly—the broad shoulders that tapered to a trim waist; the long, muscled thighs; the dark haze of his loins. He was beautiful, too, so breathtakingly beautiful in his masculine strength. She smiled, letting her eyes pay the tribute she couldn't voice.

"Paula, my sweet Paula..." The rest of Quinn's words were smothered in her hair as he took her into his arms again. She thrilled at the intimate sensation of his hard body pressed against hers, at the forceful throb of his desire.

In a sudden switch of mood, Paula laughed and twisted out of his grasp to run splashing into the sun-gilded water. She felt like a seductress, *was* a seductress. A siren of the sea. Quinn followed her, drawn as if by a magnet. He repeated the little trick he had done before, diving and swimming beneath her and surfacing right in her path. As his head and torso rose up, dripping golden droplets, he looked to her like some magnificent sea god.

"Thought you'd escape me?" he said triumphantly. "No chance!"

Her laugh was an excited gurgle in her throat. When Quinn lunged for her she playfully grabbed his head and pushed him under the water before darting away. But she couldn't evade him for long; in moments he was close enough to seize her. He wrapped around her with his powerful arms and legs, and his mouth covered hers. They sank down, then rose to the surface again, spluttering and laughing.

Quinn still held on to her, unwilling to break contact for an instant. Yet somehow they managed to stay afloat, sometimes swimming a few strokes, the warm seawater caressing their skin like silken gauze. Then, drifting closer inshore, they found their feet on softly shifting sand. They stood and kissed, their bodies locked together, mouth to invitingly open mouth, tongue enticing tongue.

Timeless minutes later they waded back to the beach and lay on the golden sand, still holding each other. Quinn idly traced a fingertip along the flowing swell of her thigh.

"Did I tell you that you're beautiful?"

"I seem to remember you did," she said dreamily.

His hand, now, was at the curve of her waist, traveling upward with slow deliberation until it cradled her breast. With the pad of his thumb he circled the nipple teasingly and smiled as he watched it tauten and peak. Paula ached with joy and yearned for him to touch her in even more intimate places. Their eyes met and held in a look that spoke of hunger and wanting.

"Paula...oh, Paula!"

"Quinn..."

They were drunk with the bliss of each other. The sand was soft and warm beneath her as Quinn explored her slender curves with a thousand nibbling kisses, whispering her name again and again. Paula floated in a dream of pleasure and happiness as she reached out for him. She reveled in the rough-smooth texture of his skin, the firmness of muscle, the hardness of bone, the spicy male scent of his flesh. Lacing her fingers into his springy hair, she pulled him against her into even closer contact. Each kiss, each new movement of his caressing hands, brought Paula to a higher plane of sensation. Moaning softly, she writhed under the delicious torment.

Urgent now to feel him inside her, made shameless by her need, she tugged at him, guided him. "Oh, yes...yes!"

Quinn was trembling, too, and she could feel his heartbeat pounding in his chest. He was a magnificent lover, generously pacing his needs to keep step with hers. They climbed together toward the summit; and then, in a final frenzy of passion, they both gave a groaning cry of triumph and shuddered into stillness. For Paula, release came in a stream of pure ecstasy.

She lay beneath him limply, spent and still trembling with the echoes of passion's joy. "Oh...oh, Quinn!"

He bent his head and printed a tender kiss on her brow. "Darling Paula. You don't know how you make me feel."

She could hardly speak for the tightness in her throat, but she had to tell him. "It's never been so wonderful before...not ever."

"I'm glad. I'm proud."

"You should be proud, Quinn. You were fantastic."

His eyes, as he gazed down at her, were soft with tenderness. "More than anything, Paula, darling, I want to make you happy."

"Oh, you do make my happy. You do!"

Quinn kissed her again, his lips still salty from the sea. His shoulders, bronzed and powerful, were sheened with sweat. After a few moments he went to roll his weight from her, but she clung to him, wanting to retain this wonderful sense of closeness. They drifted into a daze of languorous contentment, not speaking, just gently caressing each other. The sun moved on imperceptibly, and tiny wavelets lapped the shore only a few feet away.

Quinn stirred at last. Lifting his head, he smiled down into her eyes. "I've just remembered. Our dinner will be cooking."

"Oh! What's the time?"

He glanced at his watch, still on his wrist. "Almost eight, and it'll take us a half hour to get to the inn."

"Let's hope they won't mind too much."

"Of course they won't mind. The people of Provence aren't slaves to time. Where lovers are concerned, all is forgiven."

Lovers. Paula savored the word, delighting in it.

"You'd better move yourself," she said regretfully.

"I suppose I must." Quinn stood, his naked body towering magnificently above her. Reaching down, he took her hand and drew Paula to her feet—into the cradle of his arms. She pressed herself against him, her desire fanned to flames by Quinn's renewed arousal.

"You're covered in sand," he said a few timeless moments later.

"Whose fault is that?"

Grinning, he started to brush her off, flicking her shoulders and back with deft fingers. Somehow he made the task extraordinarily sensuous.

"You look mighty pleased with yourself," she commented.

"Aren't I entitled?"

"Bighead. That's enough. The sand's all gone."

"Pity," he said, his fingers lingering, tightening over her buttock.

Paula broke away and started pulling on her clothes. Quinn watched her for a moment, appreciatively, then began to dress himself. When they were both ready they started the trek back to the inn, arms entwined, her head on his shoulder.

"It's been a lovely day," she murmured.

"The day's not over yet." He said it as a promise, but the thought brought Paula a pang of wistful sadness. To say it wasn't over yet put a time limit to her happiness. It had to end sometime, and when it did . . . what?

Darkness came swiftly, much faster than the drawn-out twilight of England. Lamplight made pools of brightness in the inn's little bar where a table had been set for them. The food, served by the patron's plump wife, was simple but delicious . . . a duck cooked to a melting tenderness in a thick earthenware pot, smelling temptingly of herbs.

"This is a meal fit for royalty," said Paula dreamily. "Sheer ambrosia."

"Ambrosia's for the gods."

"Don't nitpick. It's perfect. Everything's perfect."

Later, they headed back in the boat across the moon-silvered water to the twinkling lights of the mainland. Back at the hotel, Quinn went with Paula to her room. They showered to wash off the lingering traces of salt, then called room service for a bottle of champagne. But after just one glass they abandoned it to grow warm and flat. The need to hold each other, to love each other, was too strong to be resisted a moment longer.

Afterward, Paula thought she was too happy to fall asleep. But she did sleep at last, her final awareness being of Quinn's warm body against hers, and his breath fanning her cheek.

She awoke to find sunlight slanting into the room. Quinn was standing by the open window. He turned when he heard her stir.

"Up, sleepyhead!"

"What time is it?"

"Six-thirty. And a glorious morning. Ideal for our swim."

"Great! I'll only be a couple of minutes." Paula threw back the covers and stepped out, drawing on her robe. Her hair was tumbled about her shoulders from their night of loving, and she went to the dresser mirror to brush it out. But Quinn came up behind her and nuzzled his face into the tangled, silken mass.

"No, leave it for a moment. I love your hair like this. It's so sexy."

The moment stretched. After five or six minutes, Paula murmured with a laugh, "I thought the idea was to go swimming."

"Swimming can wait."

A half hour later, in terry robes covering their swimsuits, they descended in the elevator and crossed the deserted lobby to the promenade. The morning really was glorious, the sea a scintillating expanse of silver-gilt. They swam out to the float and climbed on to it.

"Be-eautiful," Paula said with a languorous sigh, lying back on the rope-matted surface.

Propped on one elbow, Quinn looked down at her. "I agree, you are."

"I'm talking about the weather, and..."

"And?"

"Oh, and everything."

"What shall we do this morning?" he inquired. "There's plenty of time. We don't have to think about setting out for the airport until well after lunch."

The airport! A sudden chilling image entered Paula's mind of the big modern facility at Nice she had come through the previous Tuesday on arriving in France. Why in the world hadn't she envisaged this danger before? Sitting up, she looked at Quinn unhappily.

"I've just had a horrible thought.... Lady C. will be leaving from Nice today. It's the nearest airport to Monte Carlo."

"So what?" There was a faint but definite edge to his voice.

"She's sure to take the last flight of the day, like us. It would be disastrous to bump into her."

A small silence, then Quinn said, "Okay, we'll take the flight that goes an hour or two earlier."

"But there's a chance she might be on that one. Don't you see, I just can't be certain."

"What I don't see," he said impatiently, "is why the hell it matters."

There was no way Paula could explain to him. She said with a shrug, "You'll just have to accept my word that this is important. Lady C. mustn't get the least suspicion about you and me."

Quinn sat upright. His eyes were blazing. "For heaven's sake, you aren't sticking to that crazy line? Everything's different now."

"No, Quinn, it's still the same. You knew the score—I spelled it out to you. Those are the terms you agreed to when we went into this."

"But that was before we . . ."

"Why should that change things?" Her voice came out tense and brittle.

Quinn stared at her incredulously. "Can you really ask that, Paula? After yesterday? After the night we spent together?"

Paula couldn't meet his accusing gaze. She said with a heavy sigh, "Do you suppose I'm happy about the situation?"

"So change it."

"That's impossible."

"Garbage! Nothing could be simpler. You're entitled to make your own decisions, Paula. If Lady Chamberlain doesn't like the way you conduct your life, that's her problem."

"You just don't understand," she said unhappily. "You don't appreciate what a difficult situation it would make for me if she were to know about us."

"Dammit to hell!" Quinn's blue eyes condemned her. "I never would have guessed you'd be running scared of that old battle-ax, Paula."

"I'm not scared of her," she lied.

"Then how come you're acting like you are? As I told you once before, secret affairs aren't my style."

Paula swallowed hard, angry that tears were misting her eyes. "Okay, so let's finish. Right here and now."

"No!" Then, "You can't seriously mean that, Paula?"

"I mean it. You're the one who's laying down unacceptable conditions."

"Unacceptable? Because I want our relationship to be brought out in the open? That's a curious kind of logic."

"They're unacceptable conditions as far as I'm concerned. If you can't appreciate that, Quinn, then there's no alternative but for us to split up."

There was fury in his eyes. Fury and impatience and perplexity. For terrible moments Paula thought that she'd lost him. Then Quinn give a defeated shrug.

"Okay, Paula, you win. We'll play by your rules for a while longer. I'll figure out some way that obviates our meeting with Lady C."

"But how?"

"Dammit, I said I'd find a way. Just leave it with me, Paula. Right?"

Five

——

It wasn't until nearly noon on Monday that the word went around Chamberlain's offices that Lady C. had arrived. Within minutes Paula was summoned to her presence. Arabel was seated behind her massive Chippendale library table, perusing her mail. She greeted Paula with a critical frown.

"Where were you all yesterday?"

Outwardly Paula remained composed. Inwardly, as she took a seat and crossed her ankles, she felt anything but composed.

"How do you mean, where was I?"

Lady C. adopted one of her most formidable expressions, the not-suffering-fools-gladly look. "I tried to reach you by telephone from Monte Carlo a number of times, and there was no reply. I didn't give up until late in the evening."

"You were in Monte Carlo until late in the evening?" Paula couldn't conceal her astonishment. "Then how did you get back to London so soon? There's no early morning flight."

Her mother-in-law looked smug. "Lord and Lady Farleigh were also houseguests of my cousin, Princess Naomi, and they were flying home this morning in their private plane. They very kindly offered to bring me, too. Such charming people."

Paula's mind churned with anguish. If only she'd known about Arabel's plan. The scene with Quinn on the float and the bad feeling between them since then had all been for nothing. She could have flown back with him last evening from Nice airport as originally planned without the slightest risk of encountering her mother-in-law.

The whole day had been a wretched failure. After breakfasting together in the hotel restaurant, Paula had gone up to her room to get packed. Quinn had called her there to say he'd switched their reservations to a flight that left from Marseilles, which was some miles along the coast in the opposite direction from Nice. She'd at once suggested they should head for Marseilles immediately and explore the ancient city, which she'd never visited before. Secretly she'd hoped that a change of scene would miraculously bring about a change of mood between them. But it hadn't worked out like that. She and Quinn had wandered around the Old Port making idle comments about what they were seeing, but with no real communication between them. On the flight home they'd sat side by side, a mile apart. Outside her Bloomsbury apartment they'd kissed on parting, but they might almost have been two strangers.

Aware that Arabel was regarding her challengingly from across the desk, Paula inquired in a cool tone, "What was so urgent that you needed to contact me by phone?"

"It was entirely for your convenience, Paula. I wished to give you some advance warning that you'll be going to Yorkshire today. Lord Farleigh was telling me that he needs to dispose of part of his collection of Sèvres, and I was able to persuade him to let Chamberlain's handle the sale."

"But . . . you said Yorkshire."

"The Farleighs' country seat is in Yorkshire. Surely you knew that? I explained to Lord Farleigh that you were our porcelain expert, and he suggested that you should go up to Farleigh Hall for a couple of days to evaluate the Sèvres."

"But I can't go today," Paula protested in dismay.

"Indeed? I'm afraid that you must, Paula. Lord and Lady Farleigh are expecting you."

"I think I was entitled to be consulted first," Paula said, clinging to her temper.

"That's precisely what I endeavored to do." Arabel's voice rang with triumph. "What were you doing that kept you out all day yesterday, from morning until midnight?"

Paula felt tempted to point out that what she did on her own time was entirely her own business. But if, later on, it somehow reached Arabel's ears that Paula had stayed an extra night in France after the three men had left, wouldn't it look as if she'd been overly secretive? A wiser course, she judged, would be to treat the matter with casual unconcern.

"Pity you couldn't reach me," she said, and added lightly, "As it happens, I didn't get home from France until late last night. I decided to stay over an extra day at the Hôtel de la Plage."

Arabel's eyes narrowed. "You stayed over? But you said nothing about that before I left for Monte Carlo."

"It was a spur-of-the-moment decision."

"I see. And your reason?"

"Oh ... just that I felt like a break. After that rotten weather on Friday it was so gorgeous again on Saturday that I thought I'd grab my chance."

"What did you find to do, all on your own?"

Paula edited the truth. "Well, I took a boat to one of the islands just off the coast there, and lazed around. I swam...."

"You seem inordinately fond of swimming all of a sudden."

"I always have been, in the sea. But with the sort of weather we have in this country I don't have much opportunity for it."

Lady C. waved an impatient hand and reverted to the main issue. "You had better check the train schedule. Lord Farleigh suggested that you should arrive in time for dinner."

"But I told you, I can't make it today. I'll call Lord Farleigh and fix some other time." Preferably not until Quinn was back in New York! Paula hated the thought of missing a single chance of spending time with him.

"Some other time won't do, Paula."

"But I have a prior engagement for this evening," she persisted.

"Cancel it." Arabel's expression was withering. "In case you've forgotten, you happen to be an executive of Chamberlain's. So kindly act like one. A meeting with a potentially important client must take priority over a mere social engagement."

Arabel was right, darn her! Right to seize an unexpected opportunity to handle the sale of an important collection of Sèvres. And right that Chamberlain's porcelain expert must drop everything else to clinch it.

"There are other auction houses that would be only too ready to snatch this sale from under our noses," Arabel continued remorselessly. "Can you imagine someone like that dreadful man Quinn Barclay letting his private life interfere with business in the smallest degree?"

Paula was stabbed by a shaft of blind hatred. Arabel couldn't have picked a more wounding remark if she'd tried.

"Very well," she agreed resentfully. "I'll go to Yorkshire today."

Lady Chamberlain was not a woman to be magnanimous in victory. "Of course you'll go, Paula." She leaned back in her carved mahogany chair and fitted a cigarette into her long holder. "You have no option."

Back in her own office, Paula called Quinn at Sylvester's. "I really hate to tell you this," she said morosely, without preamble, "but I'm afraid we'll have to abandon our plans for this evening."

"Abandon? What do you mean?"

"I mean I won't be able to see you this evening. An important job has come up that I can't get out of."

"Oh?" His tone was suspicious, hostile. "What's so important that you're willing to stand me up?"

"That's something I can't talk about." Lady C.'s remark about Quinn came back to torment Paula. "We agreed we shouldn't discuss anything to do with our work."

Quinn disregarded that. "I'm entitled to a damned good explanation for being stood up by you this evening."

"It's essential, that's all I can say. You'll just have to accept my word for it."

"Okay, then," he said grudgingly, after a stretching silence. "We'll meet after you're through. It doesn't matter how late."

"But I won't be in London. I'll be away for the night. Maybe two nights. It all depends how things go."

His voice lashed her. "Are you playing games with me, Paula?"

"No, of course not. Why would I want to do that?"

"No reason that I can think of. But then you're not big on logical reasons for your actions, are you?"

"Please, Quinn, I'm in a great hurry. I really can't discuss this anymore now."

"When do I see you, then?"

"I'll call you the minute I get back to London. That's a promise. The very first minute. I have to hang up now."

From Quinn's clipped goodbye she knew she'd really angered him. Putting down the phone, she tried to get herself organized. First, she asked the secretary she shared with Jeremy to check out the train schedule and buy her a ticket, then to call Farleigh Hall to have a car meet her at the nearby station. Meanwhile, Paula started to clear her desk.

Fifteen minutes later, Jeremy wandered in. Taking a perch on the edge of Paula's desk, he said, "Jill tells me you're dashing off to Yorkshire, love. Can't you keep away from the guy for a single day?"

Cold fingers clawed down Paula's spine. "What in the world are you talking about, Jeremy?"

"Simple deduction. First you decide to stay over in France, and now you're dashing off for a couple of days on some mysterious mission. There has to be a man involved."

Jeremy couldn't really know anything, she consoled herself, he just couldn't. "Since you're so interested, I'm off to Yorkshire on an evaluating job. A Sèvres collection. You'll hear all about it in due time."

Jeremy chuckled. "I'll believe you. But that still doesn't account for the weekend, does it?"

"Now see here, Jeremy, I'm up to my eyebrows in work. So I'd appreciate it if you'd go away and try your feeble wit on somebody else."

Farleigh Hall was a magnificent Palladian mansion set in rolling parkland in a lovely Yorkshire dale. Lord and Lady Farleigh welcomed Paula warmly and were charming hosts. True aristocrats, they had no affectations of grandeur. Over a glass of sherry before dinner, Lord Farleigh, a distinguished-looking man with iron-gray hair, explained to Paula why he was most reluctantly having to offer the Sèvres for sale.

"What with taxation and the high cost of maintenance," he said with a heavy sigh, "it's next to impossible to keep a house this size going these days. The revenue from the estate just isn't enough to meet the expenses, even though we augment it by opening the house to the public several days each week. I can't tell you, Mrs. Chamberlain, how much it grieves me to have to sell some of the family porcelain, which was largely collected by my great-grandfather." He spread his hands. "But there it is. It's a matter of either parting with the Sèvres or selling some of the paintings. My wife and I are in agreement that Farleigh Hall without its famous paintings would be unthinkable."

Paula spent an unhappy night, missing Quinn more than she would have believed possible. But on Tuesday morning, when she was taken to the West Gallery where the bulk of the porcelain was kept, the professional in her took over. She pushed Quinn out of her mind . . . almost.

The collection was breathtaking, some of the most exquisite first-period Sèvres she'd ever seen, dating from the time when the influence of King Louis XV's powerful mistress, Madame de Pompadour, had been at its height. Small paneled paintings of flowers and birds were inset against the traditional Sèvres ground colors—glowing pinks, reds, blues and greens—with a framework of burnished gold tracery.

It was instantly clear to Paula that she'd never be able to complete the evaluation in just one day. She worked steadily, checking and cross-checking each item meticulously. It wasn't until Wednesday afternoon that she knew she'd be through in time to catch an evening train back to London. She called Quinn at Sylvester's.

"I'm coming back tonight," she told him excitedly. "But my train doesn't get into King's Cross station until 10:17."

"I'll be there. I was beginning to think, Paula . . . well, never mind what I was beginning to think. Just don't do this to me again. Right?"

"Do you imagine that I wanted to?"

"I imagine you can't have tried very hard not to."

"If you think that—" she flared, but Quinn interrupted.

"Sorry, darling, I don't mean to pick a fight. We're seeing each other tonight—that's what matters."

When, right on schedule, the train rolled into the terminal, Paula saw Quinn waiting on the platform. She leaned out the window and waved to him. His face lit up, and he started walking briskly toward her compartment. Paula's heart turned over with love. He was so tall, so good-looking, so . . . everything that was wonderful. How would she bear it if he ever ceased to be a part of her life? She thrust the thought away. In another moment the train

had halted. Quinn pulled open the door and lifted her
bodily into his arms. He kissed her fervently before her feet
even touched the ground.

"Darling Paula!"

"Oh, Quinn!" She felt a swamping relief that they
seemed to be close again, with no remnants of the cool-
ness of their parting on Sunday.

"Did you miss me?" he demanded to know.

"Madly. How about you?"

"You know the answer to that."

With Quinn holding her bag in one hand, his other arm
hugging her tightly, they walked to where he'd left his car.
One from Sylvester's transport pool, he explained.

"Where to now?" he inquired. "Have you eaten?"

"Yes, I had dinner on the train. How about you?"

"I'm okay. So... straight to your place?"

It was located in one of the quiet Bloomsbury squares
near the British Museum. Up in her third-floor apartment, Paula felt a sudden, curious constraint. It was so
overwhelmingly wonderful to have Quinn in her home. His
vibrant presence seemed to dominate her small rooms.

"I'll go and freshen up," she said awkwardly. "Fix
yourself a drink, won't you? Or make coffee, if you prefer. The kitchen's through there."

"Which do *you* want?"

She gave a little shrug. "Either. I don't care which."

In her bedroom, Paula took off the suit she'd traveled
in. After a few moments of indecision, she put on a summery dress in saffron yellow cotton. She removed the pins
from her hair and brushed it into curly waves that swung
about her shoulders. Her heart was drumming a tattoo
against her ribs. She was feverishly eager to rejoin Quinn,
yet a nervous apprehension made her spin out the moments. When she eventually returned to the living room he

was standing at her stack of bookshelves, checking out the titles.

"You look wonderful," he said appreciatively as he turned. "Just wonderful. Good enough to eat."

"There, I knew you must be hungry. Shall I get you something? I have eggs...."

"Forget about food." Quinn came and folded his arms around her, and Paula laid her forehead against his shoulder. She felt his lips burrowing into her hair, nuzzling her ear.

"You have a nice place here," he said, after several long, sweet moments.

"It suits me."

There was a brief pause, then he asked, "Is this where you lived with your husband?"

"Oh, no. Iain and I had a house at Richmond. After he died I decided to find somewhere smaller, somewhere more central." She omitted adding that their home at Richmond had been chosen for them by Iain's mother. For that reason, although it had been a beautiful Queen Anne house, Paula had never really liked it.

Quinn's embrace tightened, growing more ardent and purposeful. "Paula, I..."

With a laugh, she twisted away from him and glanced around the room. "Did you pour a drink for me?" It wasn't a matter of being coquettish. It was only minutes since they'd met at King's Cross after a space of two days, and she needed a little time in his company to come to terms with her turbulent emotions.

Quinn brought her the glass he'd poured. "Campari and soda okay?"

"Fine." She sipped the astringent drink. "Have you been busy these past two days?"

"Very. Pitching for the Webberley sale involves a helluva lot of work. I'm surprised that you found the time to get away around now, on some different job."

"Well, I had no option. But I shall need to make up for lost time."

Quinn nodded gloomily. "I wish to God we weren't both under such pressure while I'm in London. If we could only have a few whole days together, then . . ."

He left his sentence unfinished, and Paula wondered what he'd intended to say. Just that some more time together would be pleasant? Or that after a few days spent solely in each other's company their relationship would have progressed to a more secure stage?

Coming to stand in front of her, Quinn took her glass and set it aside on the bookshelves. He placed his hands on her shoulders and looked at her intently.

"I hate this secrecy, Paula. How long do we have to go on like this? How long before we can be honest and open about seeing each other?"

Paula shook her head at him unhappily. "Don't start on that again. Please, Quinn. I've told you how things have to be."

He cursed explosively. "You're making it damned hard for me, you know."

"It's hard for me, too."

"But you're the one who's spelling out the rules. You could change the situation if you really wanted to."

She caught her breath, then said evenly, "It's not a case of whether I want to or not. I just can't."

For long, tense moments Quinn continued to hold her, his fingers digging into the tender flesh of her shoulders. Then, with a low groan, he pulled her to him and hugged her close. As he lowered his head to join their lips, the silence of the room was shattered by the ringing of the phone.

"Who the hell is that?" Quinn muttered crossly.

"I'd better find out." With a sigh, Paula disentangled herself from his arms and walked unsteadily to the phone. Her voice quavered a little as she identified herself.

"Oh, good, Paula, you're back home." It was Lady Chamberlain. "I called Farleigh Hall, and they told me you'd caught the evening train. How did things go?"

"Oh, all right. Very well, in fact. What is it you wanted, Lady C.?"

"I wanted an assurance from you that nothing had gone wrong, Paula. The Farleighs will be important clients."

"You'll be getting a full report in due time," Paula said sharply. "I do wish you'd leave me to get on with my job."

"Really, Paula! I was merely taking a proper interest in your work."

"I see. Well, I'll talk to you in the morning." She hung up.

Quinn was frowning at her. "Why do you stand for that sort of treatment, Paula? If you'd joined Sylvester's, as you planned to, you'd have a much freer hand to do things your own way."

"Well, I didn't join Sylvester's," she countered. "So there's nothing more to be said."

"Arabel Chamberlain might once have been entitled to your loyalty as her daughter-in-law," Quinn persisted. "But not anymore."

"Will you please stop talking this way, Quinn."

"It's because I'm concerned about you."

"You have a curious way of showing it. You just can't let it alone, can you? You keep harping on the one theme." Why did he have to make problems, she thought unhappily, when all she wanted was for him to hold her, to love her again?

Quinn's face hardened. His voice was coldly remote. "You're offering me so little of yourself, Paula. I suppose you realize that."

She gasped in outrage. "So little! How can you say that, after... after..."

He moved swiftly, coming forward and wrapping his arms around her. "Darling, I didn't mean to sound like a heel. But you have to understand. It was wonderful for me, out of this world wonderful. But it's not *enough*. Not nearly enough."

Paula held her breath and hardly dared frame the question. "What *do* you want from me, Quinn?"

She felt a flexing of muscles in the arms holding her. It was as if he was thrown for an answer, as if he was searching his soul. "I want to get to know you right through to the core, Paula. How can I do that when you hold back from me all the time?"

"Hold back?"

"That's what you're doing. I can feel you fending me off if I dig too deeply." Putting a finger under Paula's chin, he looked down into her eyes, forcing her to meet his gaze. "I guess I want a chance to fall in love with you. I'm halfway there already. More than halfway. But being in love means total honesty between two people. And that's something we don't have."

Paula felt a cold shiver ripple through her. For an instant she was tempted to spill out everything and explain the hold Arabel had on her. What would her father have expected of her? she agonized. Would he, in order to preserve his good name, want his daughter to risk the chance of finding happiness with the man she loved? But her father wasn't here to answer that question. The choice was hers alone, and she'd made her decision after Iain's death.

For almost a year now she had suffered humiliation at Arabel's hands. Was she recklessly to negate all that for the sake of a romantic involvement that would probably turn out to be no more than a starry interlude? Quinn held out no promise for the long term.

Paula felt a sudden spurt of resentment against him. What right did he have to pressure her like this? He talked about wanting to fall in love with her, but didn't loving somebody involve trusting her? That meant having absolute and complete trust. Not a watered-down version.

She twisted away from him and went to get her drink. Her hand was trembling too much to take a sip, though. "Aren't you rushing your fences, Quinn?"

"My fences?" His eyebrows lifted. "That's a curious analogy to make. Maybe it's significant."

"What's that supposed to mean?"

"A fence is an obstacle, Paula. A barrier. There shouldn't be any fences between us. Or if there are, we should be doing our damnedest to knock them down."

"Given a little time, we'll—"

"Time," he broke in, "is something else we don't have too much of."

His ominous words quenched the last of Paula's resentment. She was washed by despair and felt hot tears spring to her eyes. Quinn noticed and came to her swiftly. She dropped the glass in her hand as she clung to him, so that it rocked before settling on the table.

"Oh, darling, I'm sorry," he said contritely as his arms went around her again. "What makes me keep saying things that are intended to hurt you?"

Her eyes were misted as she lifted her head to look at him. Suddenly she felt a flood of tender compassion. "I'm sorry, too, Quinn. Please don't be mad at me."

For moments on end they stood holding each other, and slowly their angry desperation ebbed away. Held tight in Quinn's arms, Paula felt her fears and wretchedness dispelled by the golden warmth of his closeness. They were so right together. More right, she could acknowledge to herself now, than she and Iain had ever been. She let her mind begin to shape a dream of a beautiful shared future.

Inevitably passion took over from the moments of tenderness. Their bodies quickened with longing, and their kisses and caresses became ardent and demanding. Quinn's hands paused at the back buttons of her dress, and he began to undo them one by one. He undressed her gently, with a kind of reverence that Paula found incredibly moving. And when he was finished, he paid homage to her naked body with loving hands and admiring eyes.

"You're so beautiful, Paula. So beautiful it almost scares me to touch you."

In a sudden rough hurry he started peeling off his own clothes. Paula helped him, impatient for his lovemaking. As Quinn unbuckled his belt, she smoothed her hands across his shoulders, rejoicing in the feeling of muscled strength. And when he was naked, too, they lay down together on the couch, their mouths joined and their arms entwined.

"Sweet Paula, I've wanted you so much," he whispered. "It seemed like forever when I couldn't be with you these past two nights."

"I know... for me, too."

His lips nibbled a pathway down her cheek to the silk-soft skin of her throat. Paula let her head fall back in delight, her fingers tangled in his crisp hair. There was an ecstasy to their lovemaking even greater than before. They shared a fevered need to put aside their differences, as if they could solve any problem by the sheer strength of their desire. By the time Quinn had brought her to the first shuddering peak of rapture his passion was beyond restraint. He slid into her moist, welcoming warmth, and they surged together to a glorious climax. After their soft cries of exultation there was silence except for the sound of Quinn's breathing. Paula's hands glided lovingly over his sweat-slicked back, holding him tightly to her.

They drifted into a warm daze of contentment, murmuring sweet endearments, pecking tiny kisses. Paula smoothed his thick eyebrows with her forefinger, then ran it down the straight line of his nose and sketched the sensuous curve of his mouth. He captured her fingertip between his teeth and held it gently captive, while his tongue teased around the nail.

Their blissful cocoon was shattered by the phone bell, sharply abrasive against the night quiet.

"Not again!" Quinn protested. "Damn it to hell. Ignore the thing, darling."

She hesitated, tempted. Then she shook her head and struggled to sit up, pushing him aside. "I can't, Quinn. It must be something important at this time of night."

With a heavy feeling of reluctance she reached for the phone over the back of the couch, shivering as Quinn ran a finger down the length of her spine.

"Paula Chamberlain here."

"You took your time answering."

Paula felt a blind fury at the sound of Lady Chamberlain's carping voice. "Lady C., it's very late. What now?"

"There's no need to be rude, Paula. You hung up so abruptly before that I didn't get around to mentioning what I was really calling you about."

"Can't it wait until tomorrow?" protested Paula. "It's so late."

Quinn tugged her arm and signaled for her to slap the phone down. She shrugged at him helplessly. Suddenly, talking to her mother-in-law seemed to cast a taint on her nakedness. She fumbled to cover herself with the embroidered Spanish shawl she kept draped over the back of the couch.

"It's barely past midnight," Arabel was saying. "You weren't already in bed, surely?"

"No, I wasn't in bed."

"That's splitting hairs," Quinn whispered in Paula's other ear. She turned swiftly and glared at him to keep quiet.

"I've been giving a great deal of thought," Arabel went on weightily, "to the question of venue for the Webberley sale. We've all been taking it for granted that everything but the paintings should be auctioned here in London. But we need to come up with a few really imaginative ideas to make absolutely certain that the trustees choose Chamberlain's."

Paula glanced uneasily at Quinn. Because he was a director of Sylvester's, it was vital that he didn't overhear any of this highly confidential conversation. "Wouldn't it be best for us to discuss this in the morning, Lady C.?"

"No, I wish to discuss it now. I need to share my thoughts with you. The way my mind is working, Paula, is that the Webberley villa itself might be an excellent venue. From the publicity point of view it could scarcely be improved. A great many people will be curious to see inside the villa, and the ballroom there would be ideal for holding a large-scale auction."

"Yes, well . . . this needs consideration."

"But you don't foresee any serious objections?"

"Er... none that I can think of."

"You sound uncertain, Paula."

"Well, it is late, and I've had a busy day. This is too important an issue to give an instant opinion."

"But in general you approve?"

"Yes," she said grudgingly, "I suppose so. I'm just not prepared to commit myself right now."

"Oh, very well. I was hoping to finalize this in my mind tonight. I've consulted Sidney and Jeremy, and they both seemed keen. But if we must, we'll discuss it again in the morning. Good night, Paula."

"The old dragon never eases up, does she?" said Quinn, as Paula put down the phone.

Although she felt bitterly resentful of Lady C. for spoiling the sweet aftermath of their lovemaking, Paula wasn't about to get into a critical analysis of her mother-in-law with Quinn. That was a dangerous path to take; it would inevitably lead to their bickering.

"I agree that Lady C. chose a bad moment to call," she said. "But what she had to say made a lot of sense."

"So what was it that made such excellent sense?"

Paula frowned at him. "You don't imagine I'll tell you?"

Quinn was silent, brooding dark, savage thoughts. Why did Paula put up with that dreadful woman? What kind of misguided, mixed-up sense of loyalty made her feel obliged to keep on working for her dead husband's mother? And why the hell did she let the possibility of her mother-in-law's displeasure mess up her relationship with him? He was tempted to force a showdown, but Paula was always so damned touchy on the subject.

Instead, swallowing his anger, he tried to recapture the mood of a couple of minutes earlier. But Arabel Chamberlain's phone call had broken the enchantment.

"I guess it's time I left," he said at length, confident in the expectation that Paula would protest and coax him to stay. But she didn't. If anything, he thought bitterly, she seemed relieved.

"I'll just get my wrap," she said, gathering up her clothes from the floor and heading for the bedroom. "Then I'll make you some coffee before you go."

"Don't bother."

"Sure?"

"I said don't bother."

When Paula returned in an ankle-length robe and with her hair tidied, Quinn was dressed and waiting for her. "About tomorrow evening," he began.

"I'm not sure yet about my schedule for tomorrow, Quinn. As soon as I know, I'll call you."

"You don't intend to stand me up again, I hope?"

"Of course not. At least, only if I have to."

Quinn's mouth hardened for an instant, then he smiled at her wryly, tenderly. "What we have is very special, darling. We mustn't let anything spoil it." He put his arms around her and held her for a moment, touching his lips gently to hers.

Paula accepted his kiss without returning it—not because she didn't want to, but because she wanted to too much. She was scared of letting her confused feelings spill over into an emotional scene she wouldn't be able to handle.

"Sleep tight," Quinn said as he released her.

"I'm so bushed I'll sleep like a log," she said, with a faint smile.

Bushed she might be, but her mind was too active to let her sleep. She lay in bed, listening to the muted night sounds of London outside her window, while she pondered where she and Quinn were heading. If Quinn wanted

the two of them to have any kind of future together, if he
wanted more from her than just a brief romance, then it
wouldn't be possible to go on keeping their relationship
secret. It was inevitable that sooner or later Arabel would
get to hear about them, and Paula dreaded the conse-
quences. But for the moment she would go on clinging to
the precarious happiness that Quinn had brought into her
life.

Six

——

You're really going to hate me for this," Paula said unhappily when she called Quinn from Chamberlain's salesroom Thursday afternoon. "But I just don't see any way I can spend time with you this evening."

"Not again!" He sounded irate. "What is it this time?"

"We're running hours behind schedule with our Oriental sale today. It'll be at least nine o'clock before I'm through with the paperwork."

"So what's wrong with nine-fifteen?"

"Because I simply must finish the report about my Yorkshire trip this evening. I'll be working on it for most of the night...I mean that quite literally. I'll be lucky to get a couple of hours' sleep."

"It sounds to me," he said sarcastically, "as if you're carrying far too heavy a work load, Paula."

"It's just the way it goes," she protested. "You must have those times when everything happens at once."

"I guess." Quinn's voice gentled. "But you'll be free through the weekend, won't you?"

"I hope so. I certainly aim to be."

"Make sure you are." He paused a moment before adding, "I have to return to New York on Monday."

"Oh, Quinn." It'd had to come soon, of course, she'd known that. She'd been waiting in dread for this announcement.

"Something's come up that I can't delegate," he explained. "But I'm fixing things so I have an excuse to come back to London before too long. In a couple of weeks, I hope."

Paula's heart soared again. Quinn would soon be back. His absence in New York would only be an interruption of their romance. She shut away any thought of the long-term future, of whether their relationship could withstand constant partings—even supposing Quinn could arrange to make frequent trips to London. At this point she would only think in the short term. This weekend, then some more days together in a couple of weeks. That had to be enough for now.

"One way or another, Quinn, I'll make sure I'm free for the weekend," she promised.

"I was thinking," he said. "How about spending it at my place at Putney?"

"Sounds great! I'd love to see your apartment."

"That way we won't be interrupted by constant phone calls from that damned mother-in-law of yours," he said. "So what time do I pick you up tomorrow? And where?"

"Just give me the address and I'll take a cab."

"Paula! Don't make problems."

"I'm not making problems. I'm just being practical."

She heard Quinn release a sigh. "I should know better than to argue with you. What time do I see you, then? Make it early."

"Soonest possible. Tell you what, I'll call you before I leave, so you'll know when to expect me."

Quinn's apartment, he told Paula, was the one he'd taken when he started his job at Sylvester's thirteen years ago. He'd retained the lease after his promotion to New York so as to have a convenient London base to return to on his visits home. On the second floor of a tall Victorian house, the apartment was reached by an outside staircase of wrought iron. In back, a long narrow garden ended in a balustraded embankment beyond which flowed the River Thames.

As she glanced around the living room Paula felt she was getting an insight into Quinn as he'd been in those early years, an impecunious young man on the threshold of a dazzling career. The room's aura was unmistakably masculine, but softened by a few homey touches. He had even more books than she herself possessed, with shelves rising to the ceiling on each side of the fireplace, which was a handsome feature in mottled gray marble. A divan against one wall was covered with dark green fabric and brightened by some colorful scatter cushions, and there was a brass-studded leather armchair that looked well used. She particularly admired a solid-looking yew-wood desk and a pair of bronze-base table lamps. Also an African mask on the wall, and a collection of engravings in assorted frames. All this had been purchased item by item, she guessed, as the monthly paycheck had come in. Quinn would probably have some stories to tell about his finds and the bargains he'd struck. Later on, she'd ask him to reminisce.

"You were lucky to find this apartment, weren't you?" she said admiringly. "It's really something." They'd stepped out onto a small stone balcony, which gave a splendid view of the river. Midstream, a tug was hauling a string of timber barges. To the left the sun was setting, making a delicate silhouetted tracery of an ironwork railway bridge.

"When I first moved in," Quinn said, "a place like this represented the height of luxury to me. The rent was far more than I could really afford."

Paula smiled. "And now it's peanuts to you?"

He grinned back at her. "Well, yes. But having found a place I really liked, I couldn't bring myself to let go of it when I was sent to New York."

"That doesn't surprise me. Right beside the river like this, it has a wonderful atmosphere." She gestured to the yachts and motor launches tied up in lines near to the bank. "Don't those boats look attractive?"

"If I were really living here, I'd own a boat myself. Before, I couldn't afford anything more than a leaky rowboat."

"It would be fun, wouldn't it, to set off for a river cruise right from your own garden wall?"

Quinn's smile widened. "That's just what I've planned for us to do tomorrow. See that white boat along to the right, next to the one with the tall mast? It belongs to the couple downstairs. They said I could use it."

"Oh, lovely!" But Paula had visions of being introduced to Quinn's neighbors as his girlfriend, and she wondered what she'd be getting into.

Almost as if Quinn had read her apprehension, he went on, "Steve and Brenda are on vacation in Germany, so you won't be meeting them. Which is fine by me. I need to have you all to myself this weekend."

It was wonderful, this feeling that she and Quinn had so much time ahead all to themselves. Two whole days with no fear of interruption. Three nights. With an inward giggle Paula wondered if her phone was ringing back home this very minute, with Lady C. growing more and more irritable at the lack of response.

"What's so funny?" asked Quinn.

"Oh, nothing. I'm just happy."

He took her in his arms, and held her close. "I'm happy too, sweetheart. Happier than I can ever remember."

When they surfaced from their long embrace, a summery dusk had fallen. There was a fresh tang drifting off the river. A train rumbled over the ironwork bridge, making a chain of lights.

"I was planning to take you out to dinner tonight," Quinn said, making a wry face. "But now that you're here, darling, it doesn't seem such a great idea. What would you say to eating here? Would you mind?"

She laughed. "I don't mind. Crackers and cheese will suit me fine."

"I can do a bit better than that. There's a Chinese takeout just around the corner. I could be back in ten minutes."

"How about making it five?"

"If I run."

"So, run!"

He was already at the door. "Will you set the table? You'll find everything you need."

"Sure."

It gave Paula a pleasant, intimate feeling to find her way around in Quinn's small kitchen. She sorted out two table settings and carried them through to the living room on a tray. A stripped pine table stood close to the French doors to the balcony, and she arranged the cutlery there. Before she'd finished she heard Quinn on the outside staircase, coming up two at a time.

"Did you time me?" he asked a bit breathlessly, bringing a delicious aroma with him as he came through the door.

"You're no four-minute miler, pal," she said, slipping her arms around his neck.

Later, the long night of loving they shared was like entering a world with new dimensions. Moments of high passion and scintillating flashes of ecstasy were linked by intervals of deep, comforting togetherness. Paula felt a sense of fulfillment she had never experienced in her marriage to Iain.

They slid smoothly downriver in the borrowed motor cruiser, the engine making a low-throated murmur. Paula stood beside Quinn in the cockpit, admiring the passing scene. Even a mundane structure like a power station took on a special sort of beauty when viewed across sunlit water.

They were approaching a second bridge. "Chelsea?" she queried, trying to visualize a map of London.

"Battersea. And that's Cheyne Walk over there." He pointed to the line of elegant mansions on the north bank.

"Lady C. has always hankered for a house on Cheyne Walk."

"I wouldn't mind one myself. They're architectural gems. But for Arabel Chamberlain it would be more for the snob value of having a Cheyne Walk address."

"I'm afraid you're only too right. She is a snob." Paula laughed with a trace of bitterness. "I should know."

"How come?"

Was she about to be disloyal to Iain? Paula dismissed the thought. Some things deserved to have an airing.

"That was one of the problems of my marriage. Lady C. made it plain that she considered me a far from suitable match for her son. By her reckoning, I was way down the social scale. Iain knew how she'd be—although he didn't put it to me quite so bluntly. Afterward, I realized it was why he'd wanted us to get married secretly, in order to present his mother with a fait accompli."

"I bet that made her good and mad."

"That's putting it mildly." Paula shrugged ruefully at the memory.

"She has some nerve to look down on you, Paula. The way I heard it, she was Sir Arthur Chamberlain's secretary before she married him and acquired a title."

"I don't know why we're talking about Lady C.," said Paula.

"It was you who brought her into the conversation."

"So now I'll take her out again." She moved closer and put her arms around Quinn's waist, feeling the heat of his skin under his thin cotton T-shirt. Tilting back her head, she nibbled the lobe of his ear.

"You'd better not do that," he warned.

She didn't stop. "I thought you liked it."

"Trouble is, this boat doesn't have an auto pilot."

"I'm not stopping you from navigating." Paula's hand strayed downward to the back of his thigh, clenching into its muscled firmness. "Tell me about your apartment in New York. What's it like?"

"Is that intended to take my mind off what you're doing?"

"Don't think about what I'm doing," she advised with a laugh. "Just keep a sharp lookout ahead and answer my question."

"Easier said than done."

"Concentrate!" She ran her fingertips up and down the ridged valley of his spine.

"The apartment in New York is as unlike my place here as it's possible to be. A fifteenth-floor co-op in the East Sixties."

Paula knew enough about New York to be impressed. "Nice!"

"I have some rather distinguished neighbors, too. On one side is an ex-governor of West Virginia, and on the other side a multimillionaire banker."

"Who's a snob now?"

"Ouch!"

"Touched a tender spot, did I?"

"You could say that."

They had a wonderful view of London, highlighted by the bright sunshine. The Houses of Parliament; the National Theatre Complex on the south bank; the dome of St. Paul's Cathedral with its shining golden cross; the historic Tower of London.

After passing beneath Tower Bridge they came to the dockland area, where they tied up and stepped ashore. At the famous old smugglers' inn, The Prospect of Whitby, they lunched splendidly on steak-and-kidney pudding. They sat at a table on the upstairs veranda overlooking the Thames, which was much wider here than at Putney.

Returning to the boat, they continued downriver until they were looking across the water to the graceful outlines of Greenwich. "Shouldn't we visit the Royal Naval College while we're so near?" Paula suggested. "I never have."

"Some other time," Quinn said. "This afternoon is for lazing on deck. We'll bask like a couple of lizards."

"Don't lizards bask in the sun because they're cold-blooded?"

He met her glance, and grinned. "You're right. Cold-blooded is not you and me."

On their homeward voyage Quinn produced a bottle of wine. Cold from the icebox, it frosted the glasses as he poured, and it tasted delicious. As they followed the river's course through the center of London, the lowering sun came at them from different angles. This produced a fascinating contrast of brightly lit frontages and dramatic dark silhouettes standing against the sky.

They were hungry by the time they arrived back at the apartment. As soon as they'd changed, they went for a late supper at a small Greek restaurant that was within five minutes' walk. The food was delicious, the ambience romantic. But they didn't linger there. They wanted to be alone. They wanted to be making love.

They awakened at the same time to a steely gray morning. There was the soft hissing sound of falling rain. Quinn's breath fanned her face as he drew Paula closer into his arms and kissed her lingeringly. She loved the musky male odor of his warm body and the slightly sweaty feel of his skin.

"Hi, sweetheart," he whispered, as he drew back to look at her. "Did you sleep well?"

"As well as you'd let me." Quinn's eyes widened at that, and he started to protest. Paula said hastily, with a little laugh, "I'll rephrase that . . . as well as I wanted to."

"Better. Much better. I'll go make some coffee."

While he was gone, she rose and went to the bathroom to rinse her face and comb her tousled hair. Returning to the bedroom, she heard the mailbox rattle. A minute later Quinn came back into the room bringing the Sunday papers as well as the coffee. He tossed the papers onto the bed.

"Take your pick," he invited.

Paula chose the *Sunday Times* and scanned it with a practiced eye for any news of professional interest. Quinn did the same with another paper. They sipped hot coffee and chatted idly, reading snippets aloud and congratulating themselves on having chosen the previous day for the river trip, when the weather had been fine.

"On a wet Sunday in London," said Quinn, "the options are a bit limited. Museums, art galleries...a few concerts in the afternoon."

"Don't worry. I'm happy right here for the present."

He smiled at her tenderly. "Me, too, darling. We'll wallow in a lazy English Sunday at home."

"Mmm! Sounds wonderful."

There had been plenty of Sundays during these past few months, she reflected, when she'd hated the day. Living alone, a recent widow, she'd had an empty social life that had been especially apparent on the weekends. Saturdays hadn't been so bad, but on Sundays she had sought escape from her loneliness in a frantic flurry of household chores or overzealous paperwork connected with her job. Now the prospect of a whole long leisurely Sunday with nothing to do but just be with Quinn seemed like a golden eternity.

She was into another paper by now. She folded it back and dug in her handbag for a pen.

"Let's do the crossword."

"Doing crosswords isn't one of my strong points," Quinn said. "But if you call out the clues, I'll lie back and exercise my cerebral cells."

Paula ran her eye over the clues, conscious of his foot making interesting forays up and down her calf.

"Here's an easy one for starters. Seven letters. 'Storm about return of nose ringing.'"

Quinn pondered, his fingers linked behind his head. Finally he said, "I give up."

She sighed. "Storm equals 'rant,' right? Put that around return of nose—that's 'nose' spelled backward—and you have 'resonant,' which means ringing."

He wrinkled his forehead. "That's what you call easy?"

"Here's one that's even easier. Seven letters again, and the third is A. 'Smear advertisement breaking armistice.' "

Quinn adopted a frown of deep concentration. Then he said triumphantly, "Got it! 'Slander.' "

"Slander? How d'you figure that out?"

"Well . . . a smear can be a slander, and the A fits."

"But what about the rest of the clue—advertisement breaking armistice?"

He shrugged. "Mere details. Take it or leave it."

"Idiot. The answer's 'traduce.' Truce for armistice wrapped around 'ad' for advertisement. The whole word meaning 'smear.' Simple, eh?"

"Only to giant intellects like yours." Laughing, he reached for his own paper. "I'll leave you to apply your computer brain to the crossword while I decipher the pictures in the funnies. They're more my level."

"Some people!" she scoffed, blissfully aware of his thigh pressing against hers.

Quinn's attention was caught by something he'd spotted in the paper. "What do you know! Amazing!"

Paula glanced up from trying to figure out an anagram. "What's amazing?"

"A guy I used to know has been appointed to a top job with an oil corporation. Really big-league stuff."

"Nice for him."

"It's nice for me, too."

Paula laid down her pen and looked at him. There had been a strange note in his voice. "Okay, you've got something on your mind, so spill it."

"Perceptive, aren't you?" His smile was rueful. "Ben Harlow has been a dark cloud ghosting around in my conscience for years. I've never told this to another living soul, Paula."

"Look, if you don't want to talk about it..."

"But I do," he said slowly. "I want to offload a murky episode from my past. It really is good news for me that Ben has done so well. A relief. Because way back, when we were at school together, I did the dirt on him."

"What happened?"

"He and I were both involved in a crazy stunt. Well, for the record, I was the one who thought it up. A pretty stupid idea, all things considered, but at the time it seemed too good a chance to miss."

"I'm listening."

"There was this pompous local bigwig...Sir Charles somebody-or-other—I can't even remember the man's name now. He was made chairman of the school governors, and the first damned thing he did was to present a larger-than-life-size statue of himself to stand on the main square of the campus. How vain can you get? It was to be unveiled on Founder's Day, and I conceived the brilliant idea of fixing the statue as a Groucho Marx look-alike— swallow-tailed coat, eyeglasses, floppy mustache and big cigar. So when the cord was pulled and the drapes fell away, everyone got an eyeful." Quinn glanced at Paula doubtfully. "I guess it must sound like a childish prank to you, but it was a really hilarious moment. There was a great explosion of laughter from the other boys, and from most of the parents and teachers, too. Just the headmaster and Sir Charles what's-it didn't appreciate the humor in it. They were determined to nail the culprit, and they got a lead on Ben through the owner of the charity shop in town where he'd found the swallow-tailed coat. He was given a grilling, but he refused to rat on me.''

''What happened?''

''Ben was expelled, while I got away with it scot-free.''

After an uneasy moment of silence, Paula said, ''I don't suppose it would have done Ben any good if you had confessed, Quinn.''

''It might. I could have told them the truth, which was that I'd had to talk Ben into going along with me. But the shameful fact was, Paula, that I was too damned scared. I was at school on a scholarship, you see, and if I'd lost my place there, I'd never have had another chance at a good education. It would have been like throwing away everything my mother had struggled to give me. And as for Ben, he came from a wealthy background. Ben was able to transfer to another school.''

''So the episode did him no serious harm,'' she pointed out.

''It did *me*, though. I felt like the lowest sort of heel. It put a blight on the rest of my time at school.''

''Poor Quinn!'' Paula was saddened by the picture he'd drawn of a motherless boy who'd tortured himself over a silly escapade that had misfired. ''You can't go on blaming yourself for something that happened years ago.''

Quinn's mouth crooked. ''Maybe everybody has some skeleton rattling in the closet.''

Was there a subtle question behind that remark? Paula wondered uneasily. Was Quinn inviting her to come clean about the skeleton in her own closet? But how could he know about her father? It wasn't possible.

"Try and forget about it now," she advised. "Don't be hard on yourself. Your friend doesn't appear to have suffered any as a result of what happened."

"I guess you're right. Know something, Paula, confession has given me an appetite. How about something to eat?"

"Good idea."

Adjourning to the kitchen, they dug out a carton of orange juice, eggs to scramble, bread for toast, and they made another big pot of coffee. They carried their breakfast back to bed on a large tray and enjoyed a leisurely meal. Afterward, they started watching an old Western movie on TV, but less than a quarter of the way through, their kisses and caresses became more intense and they lost all interest in the screen.

Later that afternoon, Quinn said, "What say we go out for a while and get some air? If we get wet, we get wet."

"I'm game. Where shall we go?"

"A stately home?"

"You're on."

They finally decided on Ham House, and their route took them through Richmond. It was the first time Paula had been that way since giving up the house she'd shared with Iain.

"I've just remembered," Quinn said. "You lived somewhere around here, didn't you?"

"As a matter of fact we're just about to pass it. On the left there, that Queen Anne house with the white gates."

"It's a gem," he said, and made no further comment.

To Paula's astonishment, she felt no flood of remembered emotions as she viewed her former home again. Her life there as Iain's wife seemed a long time ago.

In an amused sort of way, Paula had always been attracted by the flamboyant baroque style in which the ori-

ginal Ham House had been renovated in the early 1670s.
That afternoon, she enjoyed strolling around from room
to room and soaking up the aura of the place. Quinn was
studying the paintings.

"Old man Webberley would have had itchy fingers
here," he remarked at one point. "Although he was really
more interested in the Flemish school than the Dutch."

"Yes. Jeremy Page was saying there are some really interesting examples of Flemish stuff in the Webberley collection. He thinks there'll be one or two surprises when the
paintings come under the hammer."

Quinn, intently scrutinizing a softly lit Dutch interior,
asked casually, "Oh? What kind of surprises?"

Damn, she'd said too much. But luckily no harm had
been done. She prodded a playful finger into Quinn's ribs.
"Wouldn't you just like to know!"

He grinned. "Nobody can say I don't try."

Afterward, they went to the café and ordered a pot of
tea and a couple of sugary Chelsea buns. Quinn devoured
his in a moment, then looked hungrily at what remained
of hers.

"Oh, no, you don't," she said, protecting her plate with
her hands. "Go buy yourself another one if you're feeling
greedy."

When they walked in the extensive gardens they were
quite alone. The rain was pelting down, and the trees and
shrubs dripped forlornly. Yet they loved it. They'd have
loved fog or snow or hot, pitiless sun. Just spending time
together was wonderful.

They drove back to Putney by a different route, through
Richmond Park. Lowering clouds seemed to skim the tops
of the huge, spreading oaks, lending a mysterious, other-
worldly feeling to the scene. The herds of roaming deer,
given pampered protection now, might have been ghosts of

the wild herds that King Charles I had hunted three centuries ago.

Back home, they switched on lights. Quinn decided that a fire would be cheerful, and he went off to borrow a few logs from his neighbors' store downstairs. Paula peeled off her wet things and took a warming shower. Dressing again. she put on a jumpsuit in a soft shade of turquoise.

"You look gorgeous," Quinn commented when she emerged from the bedroom. He was crouched by the grate where a pile of logs was already flickering up into a blaze. "Highly edible, as always. Talking of food—"

"Food already?" she cut in, with a laugh. "Do you ever think of anything but filling your stomach?"

He straightened and gave her an intent look, letting his eyes run over her body caressingly. "Do I ever? Affirmative, ma'am."

After they'd kissed lingeringly, Paula turned him toward the door, giving him a little push between his shoulder blades. "Get cleaned up, and I'll see what I can pull together. Just don't expect too much, that's all."

"I was thinking we'd go out to eat, like last night."

"What? And get soaked to the skin all over again? No, thank you."

"Well," he said with a chuckle as he departed, "don't say I didn't offer to feed you properly."

His bachelor larder was pretty bare. But in the freezer Paula discovered several packets—bought, she guessed, by the helpful cleaning lady Quinn had mentioned who "did" for him while he was in residence. Triumph! A large filet steak and a box of broccoli spears. Further searching in the larder unearthed a small can of anchovy fillets. Great! She put the steak under the broiler and set water to boil for the broccoli. Smothered in red wine sauce, it would make a memorable meal. Red wine in this apartment, she then found, only came in the form of Châteauneuf-du-Pape. Too good for cooking, but why not? She searched around for a corkscrew, but couldn't see one. She went to the door. Loud splashing sounds were coming from the bathroom.

"Where's the corkscrew?" she shouted.

"Look in the desk," Quinn suggested. "Top drawer. You might find it there."

There were two top drawers. Paula pulled open the right-hand one. No corkscrew. But her glance instantly caught one of the printed words on a manila file that lay in the drawer. "WEBBERLEY."

Unthinking, she took out the file. The caption, in type-written capitals, read: "CONFIDENTIAL. PROPOSALS FOR SUBMISSION TO THE TRUSTEES OF THE WEBBERLEY COLLECTION."

Paula found she was trembling. This was dynamite. Chamberlain's was on the point of submitting its own bid, and an inside knowledge of their rival's intentions would be of infinite value.

She hesitated, fingering the cover. Suppose the situation were reversed, and it was *Quinn* who'd come across *Chamberlain's* intentions. Would he hesitate for a second to capitalize on his unexpected opportunity? Not according to Lady C.'s opinion of him. So if Quinn would seize his chances, why shouldn't she?

Instantly Paula felt sickened with herself for mistrusting Quinn, even if it had only been for a split second. She replaced the file without opening it, then hastily shut the drawer. She pulled open the left-hand drawer and found the corkscrew.

"Something's burning!"

She swung around quickly, guiltily. Quinn stood in the doorway, toweling his hair. Had he seen her at the other drawer, with the file in her hand? It didn't seem like it; he was grinning at her.

"I said, something's burning," he repeated.

"Oh . . . yes! The steak." Paula rushed to the kitchen. The steak was smoking, but mercifully not spoiled. She turned it, and got on with making the red wine sauce. But her hands were shaking, and she felt all thumbs. She was just about ready when Quinn reappeared, dressed now in fawn slacks and a blue striped shirt open at the neck. His hair was still damp and curling about his ears. He came up behind her in the kitchen and put his arms around her, cupping her breasts with his hands.

"Hey, not when I'm cooking."

He let her go reluctantly. "Smells good. What a wizard you are, darling." He picked up the half-full bottle of wine. "Shall we drink this now? I can always open some more."

"Lovely."

Paula served the food, making a lattice of anchovy fillets on the steak and adding the sauce. With the bright green broccoli spears arranged around the rim of the platter, it looked really good. But Paula had lost her appetite now, and she served Quinn far more than a half share of the food.

"Are you sure that's all you want?" he asked, lifting his eyebrows.

"Yes, I'm sure." Her voice came out thin and tense, and she was afraid Quinn would guess that she was on edge. But watching him as he dug in appreciatively, she saw nothing in his manner to suggest he was in any way suspicious of her. Even so, she still felt guilt-ridden that she'd briefly been tempted to cheat him.

Eventually Paula gave up all attempt at eating, and she laid down her fork.

"Quinn, I won't stay over tonight."

His head shot up. "Why not, darling? What's wrong?"

The huskiness in her voice helped in the lie she'd decided to tell. "I'm coming down with a head cold, I think. My throat is quite sore. It must have been from getting so wet."

Quinn reached for her hand across the table, stroking the velvety skin of her wrist with two fingers. His eyes were tender and anxious.

"I shouldn't have suggested our walking in the garden at Ham House in all that rain."

"It wasn't your fault, Quinn. You mustn't blame yourself. Only... well, I do think I'd better get home."

Quinn nodded, but said, "I was counting on our having another night together. It'll be a while before we see each other again."

"I know." Paula smiled tremulously. "But we can talk on the phone, can't we, and the time will soon pass until you're back."

"I hope to God. The way I feel right now it'll seem like an eternity." He smiled into her eyes. "Do you have a fresh lemon at home, and some honey?"

"I expect so. Why?"

"Hot lemon and honey was my mother's favorite remedy for a sore throat. It always seemed to work wonders when I was a kid. Might be worth trying."

Touched by his concern, Paula managed a faint smile. "A fount of wisdom, your mother."

Quinn's lips twitched reminiscently. "I have a lot to thank her for, don't I? She couldn't have foreseen that one of her lessons in first aid would lead to the most momentous encounter of my life. Her prescription for sore throats was to make a syrup of lemon and honey in hot water and sip it slowly. You could always add a tot of brandy to help you sleep. Now wrap up warm, darling, and I'll drive you home.''

His solicitude only added to Paula's feelings of guilt. ''You don't need to drive me,'' she protested. ''Just phone for a taxi.''

Quinn gulped a quick breath and exploded with sudden anger. ''Don't be so silly! Naturally I'll drive you home.'' Paula flinched at the violence of his outburst, and he was at once contrite. ''Oh, God, I'm sorry, sweetheart. I guess you threw me. It's just disappointment. Forgive me?''

''Forget it.'' Paula wondered forlornly if she ought to change her mind and stay, after all. But she knew it would be impossible this evening to recapture the happy mood of closeness she and Quinn had shared these past two days and nights. Better to go now, and just hope that the enforced time apart would strengthen their need for each other and recreate the magic.

It was prematurely dark. The London streets, tar-black rivers after a day of rain, shone with the glow of headlights and the red, green and amber of stoplights. There was a kind of beauty to the scene. But for Paula it was a miserable journey. She sat hunched in her seat, hardly managing more than monosyllabic replies to Quinn's attempts at conversation. Bleakly she cursed fate, cursed herself for ever spotting that confidential file in the drawer and cursed Quinn for leaving it where she could come across it.

Quinn stopped the car outside her apartment and walked with her to the front door. He held her a moment under the shelter of the porch, looking deep into her eyes.

''It's hell having to part like this. There were things I wanted to say to you, darling, things that need to be straightened out between us.''

''Straightened out?''

"We can't drift on as we were before, not after this weekend. Don't you understand that? All this secrecy and holding back from acknowledging our feelings for each other."

"Quinn . . . we can't go into this right now."

"I know, it'll have to wait. Get off to bed with the hot lemon and honey, won't you? I'll call you the minute I get to New York, and every day while I'm away." Leaning forward, he kissed her on the lips. "Take care, darling."

Quinn watched as Paula slipped into the house and closed the door. Then he returned to his car and drove away. He felt angry inside, angry because he didn't comprehend what it was all about. All day today, all yesterday and Friday evening, too, it had been pure, unbroken happiness for them both. He'd basked in the closeness they'd shared, an infinitely greater closeness than he'd felt with any woman before. And then, in the time it had taken him to shower, Paula's mood had changed. He was nagged by the feeling that there was more to it than just a sore throat. Was she resentful that he was leaving her for a short while? But didn't she realize it was unavoidable? Did she imagine he *wanted* to go away from her?

Should he cancel his trip, delay it for a few days? But his commitment in New York was too important to be put off. A long sigh racked his body. Would he ever understand women, if he lived a thousand years? Or, what really mattered, would he ever understand Paula Chamberlain? His lips curled with distaste over that surname. Paula was no Chamberlain. The sooner she changed her name, the better. Paula Barclay. He tried saying it aloud and liked what he heard.

The tires hissed on the wet streets as he headed back to Putney and his now lonely bed.

Seven

Ten days later, at eleven forty-five on Wednesday morning, Lady Chamberlain called an immediate meeting of executives in her office. Seated regally in her carved mahogany chair behind the huge Chippendale table, she seemed to be in an unusually good humor as they all trooped in. At least it couldn't be bad news, Paula decided thankfully.

With everybody assembled, Arabel glanced around at each face in turn, heightening the drama of the moment. Then she made her big announcement.

"Well, gentlemen . . . and Paula, it's now official."

"You mean we've won the Webberley sale?" asked several excited voices in unison.

"Did you have any doubt that we would?" Arabel looked smugly triumphant. "I've just had word from the trustees of the Webberley estate that they were most impressed by our proposals."

"It's an extraordinarily quick decision," said Sidney Crowe. "I suppose the various charities benefiting under Charles Webberley's will are anxious to gather the proceeds as quickly as possible. It's wonderful news, Arabel."

She smiled and nodded graciously in response to the chorus of congratulations. "I think a small celebration is in order." She rang a tiny silver bell on her desk, and instantly her secretary wheeled in a cart on which stood a magnum of champagne in an ice bucket, and a set of tall crystal flutes. "Jeremy, perhaps you will do the honors."

"Gladly."

When everybody was furnished with a glass, Arabel raised hers aloft. "To Chamberlain's, now the unchallenged leader of the art auction world." There was a ring of satisfaction in her voice, but also a slight quaver. Clearly this was an emotional moment for her.

"Chamberlain's," they all murmured. Then Sidney, as the senior executive, called for silence.

"I'd like to propose a toast to Lady Chamberlain, our own Lady C. I know you will all agree that this magnificent achievement is due entirely to her leadership. We are proud to be able to share this triumph with her." He held up his glass. "Lady C."

Paula sipped champagne along with the rest of them. But her thoughts were elsewhere. This was wonderful news, of course it was. But all the same, she felt a niggle of dismay. Where now was her justification for holding off any decision about her relationship with Quinn? He wanted everything to be out in the open, and she'd only persuaded him to go along with secrecy in the short term. Until the Webberley sale was awarded was how she'd privately defined her time limit. And she'd expected that to be way ahead in the future—several weeks, at least. Now, suddenly, she was faced with having to make a definite decision. She loved Quinn too much to bear the thought of losing him, but she couldn't expect him to contain his impatience for much longer.

She'd have to break the news about the Webberley sale when he called her from New York this evening...if he hadn't heard it already. Sylvester's was going to be pretty steamed up about losing to the smaller auction house. She wondered what Quinn's attitude would be. Could it make any difference to the way he felt about her? No! She closed her mind to the possibility. It was something she couldn't bear to contemplate.

"Paula!" Arabel's critical voice intruded into her unhappy musings. "You don't appear to be sharing our pleasure."

"Oh, it's not that. It's wonderful news, of course. I was just thinking...."

"What was it you were just thinking?" Arabel's needle-sharp eyes seemed to be boring into the privacy of her mind.

She forced a laugh and lied. "I was just trying to figure out my agenda for the next few weeks. It's going to be pretty full."

"I hope that isn't a complaint."

"When have I ever complained about having to work hard?"

Sidney made one of his diplomatic interventions. "You certainly have a lot on your plate just now, Paula, what with the Sèvres collection of Lord Farleigh's to cope with, as well. Let me know if there's anything I can do to lighten your work load."

"Thanks, Sidney," she said with a grateful smile.

It came as a relief to Paula when the celebration broke up a few minutes later. The rest of the day she worked steadily, writing detailed instructions for the staffers who would be preparing the catalog for the sale of the Webberley porcelain and silverware. She finally reached home just a few minutes before nine o'clock, the hour at which Quinn always called her. It was 4:00 P.M. in New York. The precise timing of his call was something Paula treasured. It had become the high point of each day for her to hear his deep, heart-stopping voice, and to chat with him . . . about everything under the sun except work.

Nine o'clock came and went. Ten past. A long, disappointing wait and then, incredibly, it was half-past. By ten-thirty, feeling stupidly alarmed in case he'd had an accident or whatever, she dialed Sylvester's number in New York. The operator informed her briskly that Mr. Barclay was in conference and not accepting any calls. Did she want to leave a message? Paula told her no, and hung up. At least Quinn was okay, and he'd call her when he was free.

But the evening dragged by and her phone remained silent. It wasn't until Paula was in bed, lying awake in the darkness, that the suspicion first entered her mind. Quinn had to know by now about the Webberley sale going to Chamberlain's, and this had quenched his interest in her. The dark suspicion grew during the long, tormenting hours of the following day, becoming a bleak certainty when her phone remained silent all that evening, too.

And then, about midnight when she was thinking of getting to bed, her doorbell rang. Who in the world was it at this late hour? She flicked fingers through her hair and went to answer the door.

It was Quinn, and there was an irate expression on his face. For an instant Paula just stared at him, too shocked to speak. Before she could summon any words, he stormed past her into the apartment.

"Quinn...what are you doing here? I wasn't expecting..." Seeing his dark scowl as he wheeled to confront her, she had no shred of hope left that his arrival on her doorstep meant anything pleasant.

For long moments he glared at her, his eyes smoldering. Then he burst out savagely, "What a bitch you are!"

Paula recoiled just as if he'd struck her. "Quinn...what's wrong?"

"What's wrong? Did you really think I wouldn't be mad as hell after what's happened? Did you expect me to congratulate you?"

Anger exploded through her. "I certainly didn't expect that you'd be so petty, Quinn. Chamberlain's won the contest fair and square, and Sylvester's lost."

"Fair and square? You have the nerve to say that to my face?"

"Why not?"

A crude oath ripped out of him. "You and I live in different worlds, Paula, with totally different ethics. Ironic, isn't it? I'm the one with the reputation for hard dealing. Watch Quinn Barclay, they all say...that guy's likely to pull a fast one if you don't watch out. It's true, and I make no apology for it. If I see an opportunity, I grab it. But at least I never descend to dirty tactics in the bedroom area."

"Quinn...whatever's brought this on?" she stammered, in horrified dismay. "I don't have the least idea what you're talking about."

"No? But maybe you really don't appreciate why I'm so furious. You took me for one helluva ride, lady. Am I supposed to come back smiling?" He laughed sourly. "My God, I had to learn my lesson the hard way. But at least I've learned it good and well. I won't ever again let myself be manipulated by a woman who uses sex as a weapon, that's for sure."

"For heaven's sake!" Paula cried, ice cold and bewildered. "Will you please explain to me what this is all about. You seem to think that I tricked you somehow."

"I don't *think*," he ground out. "In retrospect, it amazes me that I was such a gullible innocent as to be duped by you. All that phony reluctance about our getting together, and the whole time you were giving me the biggest come-on in history."

"But it wasn't like that. You must be crazy." Paula couldn't believe this was really happening. She said in a daze of misery, "I wasn't pretending anything with you, Quinn. I knew it would be a mistake—a dangerous mistake—for the two of us to get involved. I was genuinely trying to stop things from developing between us."

"Don't give me that crap," he said contemptuously. "If you'd had a spark of genuine feeling for me, you wouldn't have held back the way you did. You'd have been proud to let our relationship come right out into the open. Dammit, there's no law against business rivals socializing on their free time. I was just a crass idiot to fall for all that garbage you handed me about the need for secrecy."

"But it *was* needed, Quinn," she protested numbly. "You have to believe that. It really was."

"Why?" he challenged. "Why?"

"I can't tell you. Not right now."

"Why you can't tell me," he said through tight lips, " is because there never has been a valid reason. Lady C. mustn't get to hear about us, you insisted, and you sounded so damned sincere you had me believing that crazy story. Well, my guess is that Arabel Chamberlain not only knew exactly what was going on, but she put you up to it. She's been on the lookout for a chance to get back at me ever since last year when I beat her to that Spanish sale, and this was it."

"That's ridiculous."

"Is it? Be honest with me for once, Paula. You and that scheming old witch dreamed up this dirty little stunt between you. Right?"

"Wrong," she contradicted. "Stunt? There was no stunt."

"Not a detailed scenario, you mean? Okay, I'll buy that. You just played things by ear as you went along." He ran his hands over his face in a gesture of self-disgust. "My God, it must have worked out far better than you ever dared hope. You not only got me crazy to take you to bed, but I actually fell for you in a big way. What a prize sucker you played me for! You cleverly maneuvered things until you got the chance to snoop around my apartment."

"You're talking like a madman," Paula said, fighting back tears. "What was I supposed to be snooping for, for goodness' sake?"

Quinn had got a grip on his rage now. He said with withering sarcasm, "You're almost convincing, Paula, looking at me like that with hurt, beseeching eyes. Dear God, you're a smooth operator. At first I couldn't figure out how you managed it. Then I recalled coming through from my shower that Sunday evening and catching you standing at the desk. What a goddamned fool I was ever to leave a highly confidential document in an unlocked drawer! But even if I'd thought of it at the time, it would still never have occurred to me that you weren't to be trusted. I was totally smitten by then. One hundred percent." He looked at her with loathing. "Quit playacting. Admit that you found the file in my desk drawer."

"Oh...that!" She felt blood creeping to her face.

"Yes, that." Quinn's nostrils flared above narrowed lips. "It must have seemed like a godsent gift...and neatly gift wrapped, too, in a cover that told you precisely what you'd find inside. I assume you came armed with a miniature flash camera. The proposals only ran to twelve pages, so it wouldn't have taken you more than a few seconds to get them on film while I was under the shower."

"Oh, Quinn, how can you think any such thing?" she gasped, trying to keep a hold on her ravaged emotions. "You know why I was looking in your desk drawer. I needed a corkscrew."

His lips parted in an unpleasant smile. "Neat! A good spy always has a cover story ready. In a sickened way, Paula, I can even admire your ingenuity. But you might have had the decency to pay the full price for what you took from me."

"The . . . full price?"

"I mean, you should have spent that one last night in my bed. Instead of which, you just couldn't get away from me fast enough. I guess you were in such a hurry to pass on the good news to your accomplice. So you fed me a line about suddenly having a sore throat and wanting to get home. You had me feeling really sorry for you."

"Please, Quinn, you've got it all wrong. Totally wrong from start to finish. I can explain everything."

"Don't you ever give up? You'll be telling me next that you didn't even *see* that file in my desk drawer."

Paula moistened her dry lips. "Yes, I saw it. I could hardly help but see it. . . ."

"But you didn't touch it, of course? You didn't even pick it up? You spotted that important word 'Confidential,' and you told yourself that you mustn't even take a peek at what was inside."

Paula's head felt drilled with pain so that she couldn't follow the logic of this nightmare catechism. She found herself trying to be meticulously honest.

"I admit that I picked up that file, Quinn, and I stared hard at the cover," she said in a husky voice. "All sorts of crazy thoughts flashed through my brain about how valuable the contents would be to Chamberlain's. I even asked myself, if things had been the other way around, whether you'd hesitate to make use of anything you'd come across by accident like that. Then I felt cheap and mean for even suspecting that you'd cheat me, and I quickly put the file away and shut the drawer. And that's all."

"A touching little story," he mocked. "It's practically brought tears to my eyes."

"What I've told you is the truth, Quinn."

"You wouldn't recognize the truth, honey, if it came up and hit you on the head."

Paula wished that she could just feel a white-hot, blazing anger. She wished it didn't matter to her so desperately that Quinn was attacking her like this. But it did, it did matter! If she were to quit trying to justify herself, and instead tell him to get lost, she'd never cease to regret it. Quinn's contempt and scorn, the look of sheer hatred in his eyes, seemed like the end of the world to her.

"What can I say?" she pleaded. "What can I do to convince you that I'm not lying? You have to believe that I didn't cheat you the way you think. I'd never do that, not ever."

Quinn saw the tears glittering in her lovely brown eyes, and it made his heart clench with pain. But could he be sure they weren't just crocodile tears? Maybe Paula was just turning them on in a bid to win him over. But if so, why? She'd achieved what she'd set out to do, and there was nothing else she could want from him. Or was there?

Perhaps, he thought, with a treacherous stab of longing for her, Paula cared for him despite everything. Perhaps she'd been hoping her betrayal wouldn't be found out, and that their love affair could continue. But she must have known he would ultimately guess the truth, once the decision about the Webberley sale was made and the two rival bids were compared. Perhaps Paula was so lacking in moral scruples that she imagined he'd laughingly shrug it off as just the luck of the game. Didn't she know what trust was? he thought, feeling as if a knife were twisting in his entrails. Didn't she know what *love* was?

That word pulled Quinn's whirling brain up short. Love? Had he really loved her? If he had, he didn't anymore. Love was gone, trust was gone. All he had left, beneath the bitterness, was an aching void because never again would Paula share his bed.

Quinn took a step forward, his arms lifting to enfold her. He was on the brink of pouring out his need for her, of telling her that it didn't matter how treacherously she'd deceived him. Nothing mattered, except that the two of them be together. Then he hastily dropped his arms, feeling a wave of self-contempt. Was he really about to discard all his values and standards for the sake of satisfying his lust for her?

"There's nothing whatever that you could possibly say or do," he said brutally, spitting out the words one by one, "that would make me think any better of you than I do at this moment. Thank God I've discovered you for what you really are before I—"

"Is that why you've come back early from America?" she cut in brokenly. "To tell me this?"

"I didn't *come* back," he flung at her. "I was *ordered* back."

"Ordered?" she echoed, dizzy from the pain that throbbed in her head. "I don't understand what you mean."

"By my chairman. Lionel Fairhurst and my fellow directors demanded an explanation from me of how Chamberlain's was able to put in a bid for the Webberley sale that just beat our own bid."

"But why pick on you?" she asked, bemused.

He snorted a laugh. "The fact is, Paula, that all your careful precautions didn't work. One of Sylvester's staff had picked up a rumor that you and I were seeing each other."

"But how?"

He shrugged. "Who cares how? If you're so interested, we were seen at Ham House that Sunday by an antiques dealer who happened to know you by sight, and who recognized me from a press photo. He didn't rate it as of any special significance, so the little tidbit was slow to start doing the rounds. From now on, though, it'll blaze through the art world like a forest fire."

"But why? I still don't see the connection. Why should people knowing about us make anybody think that Chamberlain's had prior knowledge of Sylvester's proposals?"

He cut across her words savagely. "Unluckily for you, Lionel Fairhurst was told by the Webberley trustees that the two bids were presented in almost identical terms. The only significant difference was that Chamberlain's scale of commission was fractionally lower than Sylvester's. It's evident that Chamberlain's did a straight copying job, just playing around with the phraseology and undercutting us by a decimal point."

Paula shook her head in helpless confusion. "Quinn, it had nothing to do with me. Nothing at all. I can't account for the similarity of the two bids, except that it was just a coincidence."

"Some coincidence!"

Paula's thoughts were spinning. If any fraud was involved, it must have been Arabel's doing. She was the only person at Chamberlain's who could be sufficiently ruthless. But a coup like this wasn't Arabel's style. Hard and manipulative though her mother-in-law might be in personal relationships, she was fanatical about integrity in business.

"Quinn, it has to be a coincidence. It just has to be."

"Say it often enough," he jeered, "and you'll start to convince yourself."

"Obviously, there's no way I can make you believe me...." she began.

"Correct. You most certainly can't."

"At least believe this, Quinn...I'm genuinely sorry that our relationship has put you in deep trouble with your associates at Sylvester's. If only I could explain to people what really happened."

"What had you in mind? A kiss-by-kiss account of the seduction of Quinn Barclay? 'How I gave the poor dummy the hots for me, and then did a Mata Hari number on him.' It would make the Sunday tabloids, Paula. No question."

Her lower lip trembled. "Please, Quinn, please don't be like this. I don't think I can bear it."

"You won't only have to bear it from me," he retorted cruelly. "This is going to be the hottest piece of gossip in the trade for decades. You'll come in for some grudging admiration, but my guess is that every man in the art world will tread warily around Paula Chamberlain in the future. But why should you care about a little thing like that? You hit the jackpot! You wanted something from tough-guy Quinn Barclay, and by God you got it!"

"You're wrong, Quinn," she said bleakly. "I've lost what I wanted from you."

"What's that supposed to mean?"

It took all Paula's courage to meet his stormy gaze. "You know what I mean, Quinn. You once talked about beginning to fall in love with me. Don't you think the same thing was happening in reverse?"

She watched him ball his fists in an effort to control his rage. When he spoke, the hateful sarcasm was back in his voice. "Words mean totally different things to different people, don't they? What's your definition of that word 'love'? I remember telling you one time that just good sex wasn't enough for me. Did that give you a big laugh? It was plenty enough for you, wasn't it? A nice bonus."

"Stop it!" she cried, pressing her palms against her ears.

"Don't tell me you feel a twinge of remorse," he continued relentlessly. "That's an emotion your partner in crime would scorn. Can you imagine Arabel Chamberlain ever feeling remorseful about anything she'd done?"

"Why do you keep dragging Lady C. into this?"

"Okay, we'll leave her out. It's just you and me, Paula. You acted out a very clever charade and I was completely fooled. First match to you. So how about a replay? Sure as hell I don't intend to lose again to you."

"I think you'd better leave," Paula said, somehow keeping her voice steady. "There's no point in our continuing like this."

"No?" He sounded regretful. "Then how about our continuing more like this?"

Before Paula realized his intention, Quinn had closed the gap between them. She found herself trapped within the steel-hard band of his encircling arms. It was quite unlike any previous embrace, even in their most passionate moments. This was hateful, vicious, and she struggled to escape from his hold. Quinn put his mouth to hers and moved his lips seductively, trying to force her lips apart with the tip of his tongue. But she managed to keep her mouth clamped shut, and she made herself totally rigid. At length Quinn gave up and released her abruptly, so abruptly that she stumbled back from him, grasping a chair back for support.

"You disappoint me, Paula," he muttered.

"That was a disgusting thing to do."

"Disgusting? You always seemed to like being kissed before. Oh, well, there's my final illusion gone! Right up until now, I've been fooling myself that at least your physical response to me was genuine."

Paula choked down her anguish. "I thought you and I had something beautiful, Quinn. What you did just then was ugly. You just wanted to humiliate me."

"Like you humiliated me?"

"If that's what you're determined to think," she said sadly, "it's obvious that I can't hope to change your mind. So will you please leave now?"

Quinn shrugged his coat back into place on his shoulders and ran fingers through his hair. "Don't worry, I'm going. I've no desire to stick around. You'll pardon me for not saying it's been nice knowing you, Paula."

Crossing swiftly to the door, Quinn yanked it open. He threw a brief glance backward, and Paula recoiled at the cold blue hatred in his eyes. Then he was gone. She heard him clattering down the stairs, heard the slam of the street door. After a few seconds of stunned immobility she moved to the window. In the light of the street lamps she could see his tall figure beneath the trees flanking the square, striding rapidly away from her. Then Quinn turned a corner and vanished from her sight.

Eight

Quinn stepped blindly off the curb, heedless of the traffic, not caring where he was heading. He was tortured by his final glimpse of Paula's face, the agony he'd seen in her eyes. He wanted to turn around and retrace his steps, to hurry back to her and beg forgiveness for the cruel things he'd said.

A taxi screamed to a stop and the driver leaned out the window and swore at him. "You fool! What the hell did you think you were doing?"

With a mumbled apology Quinn stepped back, and the taxi rushed on. The driver's voice had been pure cockney, but his words almost exactly echoed those spoken to him earlier that day in Lionel Fairhurst's more cultured tones.

His summons back to London had been peremptory. The chairman's secretary had phoned him in New York the previous afternoon.

"Mr. Fairhurst wants you here in the morning, Mr. Barclay. Eleven o'clock. A reservation has been made for you on the 8:00 P.M. flight out of JFK."

"What's it all about, Sheila?" He was astonished and concerned by this unexpected development.

"Sorry, but I can't give you any details. I was just told to make these arrangements."

Quinn had been tempted to ask to be put through to Lionel and demand an explanation. It was damned annoying! He had an important appointment set for the next day, and his postponing it wasn't going to please the client. But his summons had all the hallmarks of a crisis, overriding other considerations. So, swearing inwardly, he'd agreed without protest. After calling the client concerned, he'd had his secretary in, and they'd started to clear his desk as best they could in the short time available.

An hour later, the news had come through that the Webberley sale had been awarded to Chamberlain's. So that would be it . . . a meeting of top executives for a postmortem. Understandable in the circumstances. Sylvester's had trimmed costs to the bone in pitching for that sale. Now it looked as if Chamberlain's had gone one stage further, balancing the prestige to be gained from handling the Webberley sale against whatever financial loss they might incur.

It promised, Quinn thought philosophically, to be a stormy meeting at Sylvester's boardroom in London. Recriminations and counterrecriminations would be hurled around. The thought didn't disturb him unduly; he could hold his own in any corporate battle. It never even crossed Quinn's mind that he, personally, would be the sole target.

On the credit side of this unscheduled trip to London was the chance of spending a little time with Paula. Should he call her in advance, or surprise her? He decided on the latter, and happily planned how he'd arrive at Paula's apartment with balloons and champagne and an armful of red roses.

His associates on the board had clearly been waiting for his arrival. They were all seated around the long table in the elegant room whose windows overlooked the grounds of Buckingham Palace. Instead of the friendly welcome he normally received, he was greeted by closed ranks of hostile faces. This was personal trouble! Typically Quinn didn't wait to be attacked, but charged right on in.

"I surmise from the look of you all that I'm about to be censured. What the hell is this about?"

Lionel Fairhurst had gestured Quinn to his usual seat. He cleared his throat uneasily. "The Webberley sale, of course. What else?"

"It's bad news, isn't it? But my guess is that Chamberlain's will catch a cold on the enterprise. They'll probably come to regret undercutting us."

"Unlikely, Quinn. The difference in our terms was only marginal. Just sufficient to tilt the scales in Chamberlain's favor."

"Lucky for them."

"Lucky? You call it luck, Quinn?"

"What would you call it, Lionel?"

The chairman's usually genial face reddened with anger. "I'd call it duplicity. The duplicity of one of ourselves."

"Meaning me? For God's sake! Suppose you explain what you're driving at."

"Oh, I intend to, Quinn. And we shall want some explaining from you in return. That's why you're here."

Quinn slowly leaned back in his chair. Feeling shell-shocked and totally puzzled, he nevertheless tried to appear at ease.

"Okay...shoot!"

"I have it on good authority, the very best authority, that the proposals Chamberlain's made to the Webberley trustees were almost identical in every respect to our own. Virtually the only difference between the two bids was that their commission scale was lower than ours by a fraction of one percent."

Quinn was startled. "Are you hinting at espionage of some kind?"

"I'm not hinting, Quinn, I'm accusing. Another significant fact that has just come to light, my friend, is that you've been conducting a clandestine affair with Paula Chamberlain."

"Hey, just a minute..."

"Are you claiming that my information is wrong?"

Quinn breathed hard. "Whether it's right or wrong is none of your business."

"I disagree. As your chairman I have the right—indeed, I have an obligation—to put this question to you. I'd appreciate a truthful answer. Did you or did you not pass on the details of our proposals regarding the Webberley sale to Paula Chamberlain?"

Quinn exploded. "What the hell d'you take me for?"

Another director, Sylvester's expert on Oriental art, intervened. "Let me put this to you, Quinn. Could the lady have picked up that sensitive information, unknown to you? Think back. Did you give her any opportunity?"

About to refute this every bit as vehemently, Quinn paused. The blood in his veins turned to ice crystals at his vivid recollection of Paula standing by the desk in his living room. Looking—as he saw it now—as guilty as all hell.

He passed his hands over his face as certainty took hold. Other incriminating facts raced around the perimeter of his mind, stabbing him from all directions.

"It seems," he said quietly, "that I made one hell of a fool of myself. I won't go into the details—there'd be no point. What else can I say except that I'm damned sorry?"

His frankness, his no-quibble apology, sent a ripple of unease around the table. He even sensed a certain embarrassed sympathy coming from his associates.

"There's no doubt, I suppose," the chairman queried, "that the young woman did have the opportunity?"

"Oh, yes," Quinn responded grimly. "Paula Chamberlain had the opportunity. The thought never once entered my head that I couldn't trust her completely."

"You've been a bloody fool, Quinn. What the hell did you think you were doing, taking a risk like that?" After a few tension-filled moments, Lionel Fairhurst went on, "The problem is, what now? You've put us all in a very difficult position."

"You think I don't realize that?" said Quinn. "Okay, my resignation is on the table as of this moment."

"I'm not sure that such a drastic step is necessary." The chairman glanced around the table. "What do you say, gentlemen?"

There were vague mutterings to the effect that it was all very difficult...all very regrettable. But none of the board offered a decided opinion.

"I for one," Lionel Fairhurst continued, "would be very sorry to see Quinn leave this board. Up until now he has scarcely put a foot wrong in his career with Sylvester's, and his contribution to the company's growth and profitability has been considerable. He's not the first intelligent man in history to be hoodwinked by a scheming woman, and he won't be the last. So, all in all, while I greatly deplore what's happened, I propose that Quinn Barclay should retain his seat on this board. May I please have a show of hands, gentlemen? Those in favor?''

Slowly, one by one, hands were lifted until every board member had voted in Quinn's favor.

"I appreciate your show of confidence in me," Quinn told them. "I damned well don't deserve it." He laughed shortly, feeling sick with humiliation. "That's one lesson I never thought I'd have to learn the hard way."

Despite his associates' loyalty, Quinn knew that he was diminished in their eyes. No longer would they regard Quinn Barclay with an awed respect, as the invincible go-getter. He'd have to work his tail off to regain their high esteem, and it was going to be uphill all the way.

After the meeting broke up, Quinn left the building immediately. He needed space, needed time, to get himself together. But his brain was whirling, and he couldn't assemble his thoughts logically. Memories kept stabbing at him, lacerating him. Paula's seeming reluctance to get involved with him initially...her mule-headed insistence that their meetings should be kept secret. Ruses cunningly designed to bait the hook. Then there was her sudden disappearance to Yorkshire—if she really did go to Yorkshire—to keep his interest in her at a fever pitch. And when they did eventually get together again there were those two late-night phone calls from that witch of a mother-in-law of hers. A brilliant touch that, just taking the sheen of perfection off their lovemaking in her apartment and prompting him to suggest they should use his place instead of hers for their weekend together. My God, he'd been led like an innocent to the slaughter.

Quinn's aimless walking brought him to the bright lights of Euston Road. Halting, he glowered at the fanciful Gothic spires of St. Pancras Station. Just along the street

was King's Cross, where he'd so joyfully met Paula off the
train that night.

What had his visit to her this evening achieved? Nothing! Nothing, except to leave him with an intolerable ache
of longing for her. For her sweet smile, her ready laugh;
for the sound of her lovely voice that, somehow, at one
and the same time, was both cultured lady and sexy as hell.
For her graceful walk and the delicacy of her movements.
For her tender gentleness in the quiet moments of their
lovemaking; for her sudden, wanton abandonment in the
wilder moments of passion. And all of it just a sham! How
could he bear it?

"Hello, Paula! Hey, why the long face? I'd have thought
you'd be on top of the world this morning."

Accosted in the street, Paula wished to heaven that she
could escape. She felt in no mood to chat with anyone right
now. But the dapper figure of Alistair Bennett, a dealer in
antique gold and silver, barred her path just outside the
entrance to Chamberlain's offices.

"Morning, Alistair." She summoned a smile. "I guess
I just feel a bit tired."

"No wonder, after all your exertions."

"My exertions?"

He smirked at her. "Now, now, don't try to duck the
credit. That was a really neat piece of work you pulled on
Sylvester's. They must be hopping mad about it." He gave
her a cheeky look. "I'd love to have the inside story of how
you did it. You're a very lovely lady, of course, but Quinn
Barclay is reckoned to be one smart guy. Was he an easy
victim? Or did you have to pull out all the stops?"

Paula flushed. "You've got it all wrong, Alistair."

"I doubt that." He put his hand under her elbow.
"Come and have a cup of coffee, sweetie, and tell your

Uncle Alistair all the tasty details. Did you get the secret documents on microfilm? There's a rumor floating around that Quinn kept them hidden under his mattress. Is it true?''

"Alistair, do you mind?" Paula pulled her arm free with a sharp tug. "Excuse me, but I have a ton of work to do."

"Haven't you already done enough?" he threw after her with a chuckle as she fled up the steps and into the building.

The story had already gone the rounds, Paula realized to her dismay. The various staffers she encountered on her way to her third-floor office eyed her with thinly veiled amusement as they gave her a "Hi." Dammit, she thought furiously. The vile rumor had to be stopped somehow. It must at once be made clear that there wasn't a grain of truth in it.

Paula had barely started to sort through her mail when she was summoned to Arabel's office. Bracing herself for an unpleasant scene, she rode the elevator to the second floor.

"Well, Paula?" Just those two words, delivered in Arabel's most challenging hostile tone.

"I suppose you mean this Quinn Barclay thing?"

"Naturally that's what I mean."

Paula met her mother-in-law's glance unswervingly. "We'll have to find some way of contradicting the ridiculous rumor."

"Are you saying there is no truth in it?"

Paula swallowed. "Not as far as my stealing the details of Sylvester's proposals for the Webberley sale is concerned. You know that as well as I do."

"But the rest? Is it not a fact that you have been having a sordid affair with that Barclay man?"

"We had . . . a relationship. It wasn't sordid." The pain of remembering the beautiful lovemaking they had shared was unbearable.

"How could it be anything but sordid with a man of his sort?" Arabel's thin lips curled with contempt. "I have little doubt that what people are falsely accusing *you* of, Paula, is precisely what Quinn Barclay was aiming to do in reverse. By getting you to lose your head over him, he planned to coax information from you concerning our own proposals. And, obviously, he succeeded to some extent. Sylvester's must regard it as their misfortune that they didn't have sufficient data to get their figures right. I understand that the percentage commission we specified was only a fraction lower than theirs."

"Quinn and I never discussed our work," Paula told her, trying to keep her voice steady. "He was just as insistent on that as I was."

"No pillow talk? I find that very hard to believe." A smile of malicious satisfaction crossed Arabel's face. "I hear that Lionel Fairhurst sent for Quinn Barclay from New York and had him on the carpet. Sylvester's is furious about losing the Webberley sale, and he's been severely reprimanded. Sylvester's cannot accept that the closeness of the two bids was a matter of sheer coincidence."

"Sheer coincidence?" Paula's eyes widened. "So you don't seriously believe that Quinn must have pried information out of me somehow?"

Arabel didn't like getting caught out. She dismissed her failed attempt to score both ways with an impatient gesture. "The fact we have to face, Paula, is that through your stupidity Chamberlain's has been exposed to public censure. It's not much consolation to have won the Webberley sale, if our reputation is irretrievably tarnished."

Chamberlain's reputation was the last thing Paula cared about at this moment. She said wearily, "Rumors that lack any sort of foundation usually fade pretty soon."

"And you imagine that that will wipe the slate clean for you? If so, you are under a grave misapprehension. I shall not forget what you have done. I'm shocked, and deeply disgusted, that my son's widow should be so totally unfeeling as to throw herself into a vulgar affair in less than a year of Iain's death. And with such a man! My opinion of you, Paula, has dropped to the lowest possible level."

"It didn't have far to drop, did it?"

"There's no need to be impertinent!"

"Why exactly did you send for me?" Paula demanded impatiently. "Was it just to have me stand here so you could sling mud?"

Arabel bristled. "I'm entitled to demand an explanation from you, Paula. I also want your categorical assurance that you have completely severed your—" her face twisted in distaste "—your liaison with that odious Barclay man."

Paula wished she could have told Arabel that no way was she going to stop seeing Quinn. That, on the contrary, she was proud of their relationship. Instead, swallowing her pain, she said in a carefully even tone, "We won't be seeing each other in the future."

"I should think not! Your behavior has been unforgivable, but I am going to do my level best not to let my opinion of you interfere with the smooth functioning of Chamberlain's. Let us hope that you've learned a lesson from this unsavory affair. Now the immediate thing to be discussed is your attitude toward anybody in the media who tries to trap you into a confession. You had better stick to 'No comment.' Is that clearly understood?"

Paula felt sick to the stomach with the entire situation. Sick of this vindictive woman, sick of Quinn, sick of her involvement in the Webberley sale, which had brought with it so much unhappiness.

"I think," she said in sudden determination, "that the best solution in every way would be for me to resign my job."

Arabel gave a grunt of disgust. "Oh, yes, I can quite believe you to be capable of such selfishness."

"Selfishness?"

"How else would you define the action of running away like a coward, and leaving others to cope with the mess you've left behind? No, Paula, I shall not permit you to resign. What a feast the newspapers would make of it...a serious falling-out at Chamberlain's immediately following the scandal concerning the Webberley sale. And it would be specially pithy in view of the fact that the person resigning was my daughter-in-law."

"I think you're exaggerating," Paula said. "You're overestimating the degree of interest it would arouse. Anyway, my mind's made up. I can't remain here any longer."

Lady Chamberlain rose to her feet. Despite her small stature, she made a dominating figure. "If you do quit, Paula, I shall make it my business to ensure that the blame will fall squarely on your head. It will be known throughout our profession that you were summarily dismissed by me following my shocked discovery that your father had been an unprincipled rogue. And it was immediately clear to me that you had inherited his low moral standards."

"My father wasn't a rogue," Paula protested heatedly.

"No? So how would you describe selling a painting as a Renoir, knowing it to be a forgery?"

"Why do you always have to twist things?" Paula cried. "You know how it all came about."

"I repeat," Arabel said implacably, "Ralph Grayling sold that painting in the knowledge that it wasn't a genuine Renoir. No amount of justification can alter that fact."

"But he didn't do it intentionally. I mean, not willingly. Dad was backed up against a wall. He was in a desperate situation, and it seemed the only way out."

"Which excuses a criminal act? You have a most curious sense of morality, Paula."

It was an issue they'd argued about before, when Arabel had first broken it to Paula after Iain's death that she knew about Ralph Grayling's lapse. The one and only time, Paula firmly believed, that her father had deviated from the strictest honesty in his entire life. Ever since that day, she had been forced to submit to her mother-in-law's blackmail.

But now she'd reached the end of the line. She had lost Quinn, and that meant she had lost everything that mattered. She didn't care what happened to her anymore; she didn't care if her career was in ruins. She just knew that she had to get away from Arabel's vicious domination.

"You can't frighten me anymore with your threats," she said.

"Frighten you?" Arabel's laugh rang out, a metallic tinkle. "As I said to you once before, Paula, you should feel flattered I value your talent so highly that I don't wish to let you go."

The sneering expression on her face made Paula's anger boil over. She'd endured this tyranny for too long. No matter that she had to adopt the same unscrupulous methods as Arabel. There was a weapon at hand, a counterthreat, and she seized it.

"How would you like it," she inquired in a menacing tone, "if the rumor that's going around about how I duped Quinn Barclay were to be confirmed?"

"What are you talking about? It's totally untrue."

"Agreed. But it will be accepted as gospel if I state that it's true."

Arabel's eyes narrowed. She clearly sensed rocks ahead without quite getting Paula's drift. "You had better explain yourself."

"Oh, I will, I'll explain as explicitly as you would do in similar circumstances. This is what I mean. If you carry through your threat to do a character assassination on my father, then I'll 'confess' to stealing details of Sylvester's proposals from Quinn. And I'll claim that *you* put me up to it."

Arabel gave an uneasy laugh. "Do you seriously imagine that it would benefit you, Paula, to perpetrate such a lie? On the contrary, my dear. It would only make people believe that your professional ethics are no better than your father's were."

"But you see, I'm way past caring what people think of me. All that I'm concerned with is that I'd bring you tumbling down from your pedestal along with me. So you have a choice. Allow me to resign from my job without any fuss, or else! Which is it to be?"

There was a small silence. Then Arabel gave her a superior smile. "You have a lesson to learn, Paula. If you make use of threats, you must be prepared to have your bluff called."

"It's no bluff. I mean exactly what I say, and you'd better believe it."

The two women faced each other across the huge Chippendale table. Paula felt imbued with a novel sense of power. Never before had she been armed with a weapon to equal Arabel's. And never before had she cared so little what became of her.

The supreme confidence Paula was feeling must have seeped through to Arabel. With a shrug, she reached for her cigarette holder and slowly, meticulously, fitted a cigarette into it.

"You're making a ridiculous fuss over something very trivial, Paula. If you're really so anxious to throw away all the career advantages of working for Chamberlain's and exile yourself in the wilderness, then you're welcome to do so. I just hope you realize that no reputable auction house is likely to employ someone guilty of unprofessional conduct."

"I don't care about that. Just so long as my father's name is left right out. Do I have your word on that? Your solemn word?"

Arabel didn't care for defeat in any guise. Paula could sense her mind working feverishly to find a loophole. But eventually, with deep reluctance, she nodded her head.

"Have it your way. Much good may it do you."

Leaving the office, Paula should have felt that a great burden had been lifted from her shoulders. She was free at last of the threat that had held her tied to Arabel's yoke. But her freedom was hollow nevertheless. Quinn had walked out of her life, and without Quinn in her life she possessed nothing of value.

Nine

One after the other, Paula's associates tried to argue her out of leaving. Sidney Crowe came to her office and insisted on taking her to lunch, refusing to accept no for an answer. When they were settled in a quiet French restaurant a taxi ride away, he looked across the table at Paula sorrowfully.

"I know how impossible Arabel can be at times, but you really shouldn't let her get to you, my dear. Not to this degree. You belong at Chamberlain's along with the rest of us. You play a vital role in the organization. Please reconsider your resignation."

Paula shook her head. "Thanks for caring, Sidney. I appreciate your concern. But my mind is made up."

He sighed. "I suppose she gave you a hard time about your friendship with Quinn Barclay?"

"A hard time is right."

"She seizes any excuse to harass you, Paula, you know that. But you can always handle Arabel. She doesn't mean half the things she says to you. Not seriously."

"She did this time, Sidney. Every nasty word."

"Arabel's damned wild, of course, about the ridiculous rumor that's going the rounds. We're all of us upset about it, naturally, and it must be very distressing for you." Sidney released a sigh. "Unfortunately it would be counterproductive for Chamberlain's to issue a denial. The only way for us is to adopt a dignified attitude and ride out the storm. Given a little time, the whole thing will blow over."

"I guess. But what's just happened is only part of why I'm leaving, Sidney. I've thought about quitting Chamberlain's ever since Iain died."

He pursed his lips and looked at her seriously. "To be candid, Paula, I didn't expect you to stay on in those early days. But I was very glad you decided to, of course. I gather you were considering joining Sylvester's at one point."

"Who told you that?" she asked in surprise.

"Oh, these things have a way of getting around. So, my dear, what will you do now?"

"I don't know. I haven't given it a lot of thought."

"Well, whatever you decide to do, make sure you don't waste your talent."

She smiled. "I'll try not to."

"We'll all be rooting for you, Paula. And if you ever need a favor, you know where to reach me. I mean that."

"Thank you, Sidney. I really appreciate that. You've always been a very good friend to me." She pressed his hand where it lay on the table in a gesture of affection.

Sidney sobered again. "I hear that Quinn is back in New York already. Rumor has it that you two have split up."

"Rumor has it right, for once."

He shook his head sadly. "Such a pity. You and Quinn would have made an ideal pair."

"Oh, well, that's life!" said Paula, making a feeble attempt to sound uncaring.

It was a strange experience for Paula to have no office to go to, no job to exercise her brain cells. She knew it was unhealthy to have nothing special to do, but for the first couple of weeks after quitting Chamberlain's she just couldn't find the energy or interest to make plans for her future.

She refused to stay home and mope, but she had no urge to seek the company of her friends. Instead, she made solitary visits to some of the lesser museums in London, which, because they didn't make a special feature of ceramics or silverware, she had missed out on before. One day, Paula headed for Thomas Carlyle's house in Chelsea. But before going inside she paused a moment to glance across the River Thames. With a sudden rush of memory, she thought of that perfect day she'd spent with Quinn when they'd cruised down London's waterway. She'd felt happier that day than ever before in her life.

A lump formed in her throat, and tears stung behind her eyelids. She was in no mood for cultural pursuits. She continued walking, aimlessly, and in a couple of minutes she came to King's Road with its cosmopolitan crowd. A crowd to lose herself in. Or so she thought, until she saw a well-known dealer in Oriental porcelain coming toward her. Paula pretended not to notice him and dived into a boutique.

Next day she rented a car—owning one in central London was more trouble than it was worth—and set off on a minitour, heading westward. She rubbernecked at Blenheim Palace near Oxford, birthplace of Sir Winston Churchill. Then she visited Bath, the entire city a museum, from Roman times to Regency. She stayed at small, inexpensive guest houses deep in the countryside. And in their peaceful, homey comfort, her shattered emotions began to heal.

A new job—that was what she needed now. It wasn't a question of money; the sale of the house at Richmond, plus an insurance policy, had left her reasonably well provided for after Iain's death. But she wasn't cut out for a life of idleness.

So, after only five days, Paula cut her trip short and returned to London. If she couldn't find a satisfying post in her own profession, she decided, then she'd do something totally different. One thing was for sure, her time of moping was over.

She arrived home late in the afternoon of a scorching day toward the end of August. As she drove into the city, the workers going home looked weary and limp. Near her apartment, the leaves of the plane trees in the square were droopy and dusty.

After a reviving cup of tea, Paula began to switch around the furniture in the apartment. She needed change; she needed to get away from reminders of the past. Pushing the big couch to a new position facing the window brought her a pang. It was where she had lain with Quinn on the night of her return from Yorkshire. Afterward, they had remained close, holding each other . . . until the interruption of Arabel's phone call had shattered their wonderful mood of harmony.

As if on cue, the phone rang now. Paula jumped at the sound; then answered it.

"Paula Chamberlain here."

Silence. Not heavy breathing or anything like that. Just silence.

"Who is this?" she asked.

Paula heard a click, then the dial tone started. Shrugging, she replaced the phone. Someone with a wrong number who didn't have the courtesy to apologize. Even so, the call left her feeling on edge.

A half hour later—less—the doorbell chimed. What now? She went to the door and found Quinn standing outside. The shock of seeing him there jolted through her entire body.

"Hello, Paula," he said, his eyes scanning her face.

She found her voice and asked, "Was that you who phoned just now without speaking?"

"That was me. I've come by several times and found you not at home. The people in the apartment downstairs told me you were away, and they didn't know when you'd be back. I've been calling your number constantly these past two days, then finally you answered."

"But why did you just hang up like that?"

"In case you told me not to come over. You might have gone out again to avoid me. Sorry if the anonymous call alarmed you."

She shrugged. "It just seemed a bit odd. Anyway, Quinn, what do you want?"

"To talk to you."

"What's to talk about?" she asked wearily.

"Us."

"There is no us."

"There is…there has to be. I have things to say to you."

She shook her head at him emphatically. "You already said plenty. Far too much."

"Please, Paula…"

"I suppose you'd better come in," she muttered ungraciously, and stood aside for him to enter.

In her living room, Quinn looked around. "You've changed things around, Paula."

She found it unnerving to be standing so near him. This hot summer evening he was wearing a short-sleeve shirt, open at the neck. The skin of his forearms was deeply tanned, the sprinkling of hairs looking a pale bronze in contrast. All her sensors were acutely attuned to him, picking up his radiating warmth, his unique male scent, the strong, emotional vibrations that seemed to crackle across the gap between them.

"So I've changed things," she said in a flat voice. "Big deal."

"I think I liked it better the way it was before."

"Too bad. But the way you like my living room is immaterial. I don't anticipate that you'll ever be seeing it again."

Quinn's eyes were somber as they met hers. They held a look of appeal. "Paula, I've flown from New York especially to see you."

"You shouldn't have bothered. It's a waste of time and money."

"I had to come," he said. "I had to straighten things out between us."

Paula flared at him. "Things *are* straight between us...now. They weren't before, because I was stupid enough to believe that you really cared about me. But I know now how shallow your feelings must have been if you didn't trust me. If you would seriously believe that I'd have..."

"I was wrong about that, Paula. Terribly wrong. I know that now, and I'm desperately sorry."

"Now he says it! You're too late, Quinn. Three whole weeks too late."

Quinn frowned, clearly uncertain how to handle this situation. "I hear that you've resigned your job at Chamberlain's."

"You heard right."

"It's something you should have done months ago. Working for that damned woman was a bad mistake. So what are you doing now?"

"That's not your concern."

He gave her an exasperated look. "I've come to London to admit that I was wrong, Paula. To apologize very humbly. What more do you expect?"

"Nothing. I don't want anything from you, Quinn. Just keep out of my life, okay?"

"You can't really mean that," he said. "Not after what we had between us."

"That episode belongs to the past. It's finished and over. It's history."

"Not for me, Paula. I can't forget what we had as easily as you seem able to do."

"Forget?" A choky feeling caught her throat. "I'm forgetting nothing. I thought they were good times, too, but then you shattered all my rosy-hued illusions. You made the most vile accusations against me, and..."

"I told you, I made a terrible mistake about that."

"But you believed it at the time. You actually believed what you accused me of. That's what hurt so much...that you could really think I was capable of cheating you like that. You had no faith in me, Quinn. No trust in me."

"How much trust did you have in me?" he countered.

Paula gave him a startled glance. "I never mistrusted you."

"Yes, you did. Right from the start. You kept harping on about the need for secrecy, but you never gave me a sound, logical reason why Arabel Chamberlain mustn't get to hear about us. You didn't trust me enough to tell me what the problem was."

"No, you're wrong. It wasn't a matter of not trusting...." But Paula's rebuttal died in her throat. It was a lie. To have explained her reticence concerning their romance to Quinn would have required relating the whole story about her father. But once before she'd done that; she'd confided in her husband. And Iain had betrayed her by immediately disclosing her confidence to his mother. She hadn't dared to take the risk of something similar happening again. She'd believed at the time that she loved Quinn, *knew* that she loved him. Yet that complete trust between a man and a woman that loving should bring had been lacking.

Quinn ignored her denial. He could read the evasive message of her eyes. "Now that you've quit Chamberlain's," he said, "you can tell me why it was so important to you that we kept our relationship a secret."

"No, I can't do that."

"Dammit, Paula, why do you persist in keeping up this barrier? Things could be so good between us, so wonderful. We've already proved that."

"Until it came to the crunch," she said bitterly. "Then you started calling me vile names."

"We've been through all that."

"Which doesn't put things right. Nothing ever will."

"Why say that?" he demanded. "Why deliberately throw away all that magic we shared? I won't let you throw it away, Paula."

"The choice isn't yours to make."

There was a tense, stretching silence. The sultriness of the hot summer evening seemed to have invaded the room, and Paula felt starved of air. Her pulses were throbbing and her breathing was fast and shallow. For long moments they looked at each other, then Quinn took a step toward her. She backed off, and he angrily swung on his heel and went to stand at the window.

"The other time I was here, it was dark," he said quietly, after a lengthy hesitation. He turned back to face her. "The light from the street lamps was flickering through the trees. It was good, wasn't it? Aside from the interruptions."

"Which you afterward imagined were all a part of some devious plot."

This time Quinn moved too quickly for Paula to evade him. He held her by the shoulders and looked into her eyes with a deep, penetrating gaze.

"Paula...it makes no sense to keep raking over old hurts. We both of us made mistakes. So why can't we put the past behind us? Just hold on to the good times, and forget all the rest."

"How can you expect me to do that?" she said with an aching sadness. "What happened, happened. It's something I can't ever forget."

"Okay, forget about forgetting. But let's make a fresh start now. I'm Quinn Barclay, you're Paula Chamberlain. Let's pretend we've just met. Then we can take it from here."

"You amaze me, Quinn, you really do. Are you seriously suggesting this as a possibility?"

"Why not? It's a simple matter of wanting. Of making it possible."

"Perhaps it is, from your male viewpoint. But for me that's too easy. I can't rule a line across the past and just start over. The past and the present and the future are all parts of the same continuing pattern of my life.''

''Which includes the good times you and I shared,'' Quinn reminded her insistently. ''However you choose to view your life, Paula, there's still a logical reason for us to make the magic between us happen again. It *can* happen—you know that. You've only to look in your heart.''

A tremor passed through her. She felt exhausted, her nerves in shreds. ''Quinn, please let me go,'' she said in a hoarse voice.

It was a plea that went far beyond the simple meaning of the words. She was begging him for release from a far deeper hold than the mere grip of his hands on her shoulders. She'd thought she had been liberated from Quinn's thrall through the sheer white heat of her anger against him. But she knew now how quickly anger could lose its intensity.

''Let me go,'' she repeated faintly.

Instead, Quinn drew her closer against him. As his arms folded around her, Paula felt engulfed by the vibrant warmth of his body and the remembered comfort of his embrace. She just, but only just, found will enough to turn her face away when he brought his mouth close to hers.

''You shouldn't have come,'' she whispered.

''I *had* to come.''

''When will you be returning to New York?'' she asked. How soon? she meant. How soon before she would be free of him, with an ocean between them?

''That depends.''

''On what?''

''On you. Now that you've quit Chamberlain's, you could come to New York with me.''

Quinn felt Paula's start of surprise. He had surprised himself. Up until this instant, his only thought had been to

mend fences with Paula. Just that. Get back to where
they'd been. With her so implacably hostile, he'd begun to
feel desperate. But what exactly was he now suggesting?
His mind again skimmed around the idea of marriage. But
his instincts warned him that it was too soon to mention
marriage . . . certainly for Paula, even if not for himself.

"Why not come to New York?" he urged. "The way I
heard it, you're not yet fixed up with another job, and
maybe it would suit you to get right away from London.
The Americans have a great respect for talent. There are
numerous opportunities for somebody with your qualifi-
cations, Paula."

"Even," she said with bitterness, pulling away from his
hold, "somebody believed to have criminal tendencies?"

"Oh, for God's sake," he said impatiently. "Who really
believes that?"

"Lots of people. Almost everybody. Just as you yourself believed me guilty of stealing secrets from you up until . . . when, Quinn? Or maybe you still do believe that,
deep down."

"No," he denied vehemently. "Of course I don't. I keep
telling you, I know now that I made a ghastly mistake."

"How can you be so sure?" she challenged him impul-
sively. "What makes you so certain of it?"

Paula knew the kind of words she longed to hear him
say. I'm sure, darling, because it's unthinkable you could
ever be a cheat. I'm sure because I love you and I have total trust in you, total faith in you. I only ever mistrusted
you for a brief time when I was overwhelmed by the ava-
lanche of criticism and abuse that hit me all of a sudden,
so that I couldn't think straight.

But what Paula actually heard were different words. As
she listened, her initial disappointment turned to dismay,
then to an icy wretchedness. Amazingly, from the way

Quinn spoke he actually seemed to imagine that she should be pleased, as if he were telling her some good news.

"I've been making a few inquiries, Paula. I needed to satisfy myself, but it wasn't easy to get any authentic information. In the end, I decided to approach Sidney Crowe."

"Sidney?"

"Well, I've known him for quite a few years. His son, Malcolm, and I were at university together and I was invited to the Crowes' place a couple of times. Then Malcolm was killed in a climbing accident, but I used to meet Sidney around from time to time in the course of our work. He and I have always liked and respected each other."

"I see," said Paula through tight lips. "And what exactly did you ask Sidney?"

"I put a straight question to him. Had there been any sort of underhand maneuverings behind the Chamberlain's bid for the Webberley sale? I'm not suggesting Sidney could have admitted it to me if there had been, but his denial was so emphatic that I knew he was telling the truth. Other people maybe wouldn't have believed him; they'd have imagined he was just defending his own firm. But I know Sidney Crowe well enough to be able to accept his word absolutely." Quinn broke off, and asked, "What's up, Paula? Why are you staring at me like that?"

"My God, you really don't know, do you?"

"I can't see why you should suddenly get mad. You don't seem to understand what I'm telling you."

"Oh, I understand, Quinn. I understand only too clearly. You're saying that you were happy to take Sidney Crowe's word for something when you couldn't accept mine. That's rich!"

"You're twisting things, Paula. I didn't mean it like that. But Sidney wasn't personally involved, the way you were."

"And that's an adequate reason for mistrusting me?" She was boiling with indignation. "You believe that I'm capable of lying to you and cheating you if it should happen to be to my personal advantage, and you're telling me now that it's all okay between us because on this particular occasion you've managed to find out that I didn't lie and cheat. The only problem with that, Quinn, is that you're applying your own contemptible standards of ethics to me."

"Paula, I'm sorry...."

"So you damned well should be. But just saying you're sorry doesn't alter anything."

"For pity's sake, Paula! You're overreacting like crazy. I don't know why you have to be like this."

"No, you don't, do you? You really don't know. That comes over loud and clear. It seems to me, Quinn, that we're AM and FM, for all we connect."

"We weren't when we were together," he reminded her in a tone of reproach. "I came to see you with the best of intentions, all the way from New York."

"So you said before. Does each additional mile you traveled make your intentions that much nobler? Maybe a twelve-thousand-mile trip from Sydney, Australia, might have won me around. But you'll never know the answer to that, will you?"

"Take it easy, Paula, there's no need to be sarcastic. I didn't mean for you to take what I just said the way you did. I just want to get things right between us."

"Forget it, because you never will. Things never were right between us. We merely thought they were, but we were deluding ourselves." She faced him with her eyes blazing. "I think you imagine that good sex is all that's needed for a successful relationship. But you're so wrong—sex is only the tip of the iceberg."

"If you and I didn't have the whole iceberg," Quinn said bitterly, "you can ask yourself why we didn't."

"What's that supposed to mean?"

"There was always a barrier between the two of us, Paula, and it was entirely of your making. Right from the start, I wanted us to be straightforward and open about our seeing each other. It was you who wouldn't have that . . . you who made our affair something furtive and secretive."

Paula was lost for an answer. All she could do was to mutter defensively, "I had a good reason for acting the way I did."

"So you keep on telling me. I'm merely pointing out that if we're into a discussion about trusting and not trusting each other, you have at least as much to apologize for as I do."

"I put my trust in someone once before," she said defensively, "and it brought me nothing but problems."

Quinn gave her a measuring look. "Your husband?" She hesitated. Then, "Yes, Iain."

"Tell me about it."

Paula laughed mirthlessly. "I'm hardly likely to do that now, am I, when I wouldn't before?"

"Why not? I told *you* something I'd never told to anybody else. The time has come for you to make a confession to me."

"No, never!"

His eyes widened. "Never? That's a very revealing statement. The way I interpret it, that means that even when it looked as if you and I really had something good going, a relationship that might have become permanent, you still envisaged going through life holding out on me?''

"I never though of anything permanent between us," she lied in self-justification.

"Didn't you? I did! Not at first, I admit that. I've always shied away from getting tied down in a long-term relationship. But it wasn't long before I began to think of nothing else but having you permanently in my life. And I believed it was the same for you."

"Well, you thought wrong!"

"Paula . . . tell the truth."

Fresh fuel was added to her anger by a feeling of hopelessness, of bitter despair. "I'll tell you the truth, Quinn. I want you to go away and leave me alone. I'll be glad if I never need to set eyes on you, ever again. How's that? Is it plain enough for you?"

There was a look of dazed incredulity in Quinn's eyes, then he burst out furiously, "Okay, Paula, I'll get out of your life. You're too hard a woman for me. Too damned hard and unforgiving." He hesitated, looking at her as if there was something else he wanted to say. But then he just shook his head and made for the door.

He didn't even say goodbye. His departure was so swift that Paula was left reeling with the shock of it. She stood motionless in the center of the room, feeling so sick and faint that she was afraid she was going to pass out.

"What have I done?" she whispered. She knew the answer, though. She might just as well have severed one of her hands or a foot. She would never be a whole person again. Not ever.

Ten

It was Jeremy Page who drew Paula's attention to the job. He called her at home one evening while she was writing some query letters.

"Hi, there, sweetie," he said breezily. "How're things with you?"

"Could be worse, Jeremy."

"Like that, is it? Well, cheer up. It's a great day tomorrow, and all that jazz. Now, are you anywhere near to fixing yourself up with a new j-job?"

"Not yet. I'd hate to get a name for being overly picky, on top of everything else. But I see no point in jumping into something that doesn't really stretch me. Some of the new jobs I've been offered...well, quite frankly and without meaning to boast, I could handle them with both hands tied behind my back."

"Sure you could. Be as picky as you like. You need something you can make a b-brilliant success of. That'll knock 'em all for a loop."

"Wouldn't I just like to do that! The problem is, there aren't any nice juicy plum jobs waiting to be plucked from the tree."

"Aha!" he said triumphantly. "That's j-just where you're wrong."

"Jeremy...do you really mean that? Do you know something?"

"The Barrington Museum up in Northumberland."

"The Barrington? How would they be able to use me? They don't have any quantity of ceramics or silverware. And the little they do have isn't notable."

"It isn't a matter of what they have, but what they're about to get. Some immensely rich guy named Arthur Matlock, who made his pile out of building highways—no, Paula, I'd never heard of him, either—has decided to earn his place in the history books by making a dazzling dona-tion for the public good. Turns out he's buying the Chas-serlaux porcelain collection lock, stock and barrel. Eight million it's costing him, and it'll be handed over to his lo-cal museum. Which—luckily for them—happens to b-be the Barrington."

"I've heard nothing of all this."

"It's been kept under wraps up until now. But the news will break anytime. I know the guy who runs the Barring-ton Museum. Bertram Gideon. I negotiated some nice Louis XV pieces for him a while back. Anyway, I m-mentioned your name to him, Paula, and he's extremely interested. With an acquisition like the Chasserlaux col-lection, he'll need a really prime-grade talent to organize the new department."

"I wonder..." Paula was thinking aloud. "Northumberland."

"A beautiful part of Britain," said Jeremy, doing a hard sell. "Wide-open spaces, the g-great outdoors, lots of away-from-it-all. How I envy you."

"Huh! You'd be lost away from London, Jeremy. Still, this is really interesting. As a stopgap, I mean. They wouldn't be offering a permanent position, anyway."

"Bertram would be thankful to have someone of your caliber, Paula, for as long as you're willing to give him. Three months of your time would get his new department pointing in the right direction. A couple of years would really get it humming."

"I'm definitely tempted. I guess I could rent this apartment."

"Of course you could. Slap in the heart of stylish B-Bloomsbury! If I had a few thousand a year to spare, I could set up a sexy lady friend very nicely there."

Paula laughed. "Who are you trying to impress? You'd pine away if you couldn't get home to Myra's cooking every evening. Not to mention Myra herself. You know it, she knows it, I know it...."

"Have a heart, sweetie. Would you strip a man of his hard-won reputation?"

She laughed again. "Anyhow, thanks a million for the tip, Jeremy. I'll call Bertram Gideon first thing tomorrow and see what he has to say."

Paula's phone call the next morning led to her taking a trip north the following day.

She felt an immediate affinity with Northumberland's wild countryside of rolling, wavelike hills, and its sweeping sense of history. The great classical mansion that now housed the Barrington Museum looked across this landscape to the distant outline of Hadrian's Wall, where the

Roman legionnaires had defended the British province against marauding Picts from the north. Standing at a window with Bertram Gideon, a scholarly, stooped man of about sixty-five, with a quaint habit of shooting penetrating glances over the top of his horn-rimmed glasses, Paula reflected on how little the scenery must have changed since those ancient times.

"I like it here," she told him simply.

"I'm glad, my dear. I make no bones about it. I'm very keen for you to join us. You'll be a big asset to the Barrington." He treated Paula to another of those slightly unnerving glances. "Chamberlain's loss will be our gain."

"You don't object to the reputation that comes along with me?"

He shrugged his spare shoulders. "Rumors! I prefer to take people at my own personal evaluation of them. Now...listen to my plans, Mrs. Chamberlain...Paula. I want to allocate this entire wing to the new ceramics department. The exhibits we have here now are miscellaneous pieces that can easily be accommodated in other sections of the museum. You'll have space to display the Arthur Matlock Collection—as it will in future be called—as such a fine collection deserves to be displayed. And more than adequate funds at your disposal."

They agreed that her initial contract would be for a period of six months. "I'd really like to tie you down for longer than that," Bertram said, with a wry twist of his lips, "but I'd hate a contract to stand in your way when the time comes, as it surely will, that you want to return to a mainstream career."

The windswept hamlet of Barrington was clustered around the entrance gates of the big house. Paula had taken a room at the small, seventeenth-century Woolpack

Inn. Great oak beams supported the low ceiling, and the cream-washed walls leaned at odd angles. Her bed, spread with a patchwork quilt, had shining brass rails with a knob at each corner. But there were modern amenities, too; a well-fitted bathroom adjoined the bedroom. Downstairs, she had the use of a comfortable lounge with, on these chilly northern evenings, a big log fire. Her meals she ate in the quaintly pretty dining room, with ample, homey fare prepared by the landlady herself.

Staying at the inn, Paula was relieved of the daily chore of housekeeping, which suited her for the present. Maybe later she'd find a cottage to rent, but she was in no hurry. Her London apartment had been snapped up on a six month lease almost as soon as it had been listed by the agency by a pleasant American couple, both working in advertising.

Her new job, which by coincidence she'd started on the anniversary of Iain's death, lacked the day-to-day challenge and nerve-tingling excitement of the auction world. But in recompense it gave Paula something else, a sense of continuity. Instead of having an endless succession of art treasures pass through her hands and disappear, the porcelain in her charge at the Barrington would stay with her, to be loved and cherished.

Each day now, security vans arrived at the museum loaded with crates of valuable porcelain. Paula supervised the unpacking in one of the large basement storerooms that had been allocated to her department. Here, at the moment, was where she spent most of her time, meticulously inspecting and annotating each magnificent piece. Meanwhile, upstairs, the exhibition rooms were being renovated according to her instructions.

One afternoon toward the end of September, Paula was checking some Italian majolica that had just arrived when a call from the desk in the front hall informed her that someone was asking to see her.

"Who is it, Mavis?" she queried, her mind elsewhere.

"Er... Mr. Barclay. Mr. Quinn Barclay."

"Oh..." A frozen moment, then the basement room started to gyrate.

"Mrs. Chamberlain, are you there? Do I send Mr. Barclay down, or will you come up?"

"No...no, I can't see him."

"He's driven from London especially, he says."

"I can't help that. Tell him to go away."

"Oh, very well." Mavis managed to put surprise, disapproval and resentment into her voice. The phone was banged down.

Paula was far too shaken to return at once to the job at hand. Her thoughts were whirling—anger and pain, puzzlement, excitement and hope. What was happening upstairs in the front hall? Was Quinn making a scene at this moment? Would he insist on seeing her? What did he want, anyway? Why had he come back to see her after the way he'd slammed out of her apartment five weeks ago? Maybe she ought to see him....

Before she could have second thoughts she dialed the front desk.

"What happened about Mr. Barclay, Mavis?"

"I gave him your message, just like you told me."

"And?"

"He tried to argue with me. But I said you'd been quite definite about not seeing him."

"You mean, he left?"

"Yes, Mrs. Chamberlain. That was what you wanted, wasn't it?"

"Didn't he leave any message?"

"No, no message. He looked very angry, though."

"I see...." Paula hung up thoughtfully.

For the last two hours of the afternoon, she achieved nothing useful. It was as much as she could do to pretend to be working. Somehow, she couldn't visualize Quinn meekly giving up and going away, once he'd made up his mind to see her. She felt her nerves stretched to the breaking point as she considered the possibilities of what further action he might take. She was wishing now that she'd agreed to see him, after all. It would have been better to know what he wanted to say to her—whatever it was—than to be tormented by this uncertainty.

Paula quit work early, having decided that she'd spend a little time strolling in the museum's spacious grounds before heading home for the inn. Except when it was raining, she didn't use her recently acquired car to get to work. It was a pleasant half-mile walk. Fifty yards along the quiet, grass-verged village street and the rest of the way up the museum's private driveway that curved through elegant parkland studded with English oaks. Today, Paula extended her homeward journey by making a leisurely circuit around the perimeter of the large, serpentine lake. She came to no conclusions, made no decisions, but the peacefulness of the scene as she watched some swans gliding serenely across the still water somehow had a soothing effect. It wasn't until the setting sun was catching just the topmost tips of the trees that she reluctantly quickened her steps and headed for the entrance gates.

As she drew near, she heard a car door slam. A moment later a tall figure appeared in the gatehouse archway. Paula faltered almost to a stop. Then, scorning her lack of courage, she walked steadily to meet Quinn.

"I thought you'd been given a message that I wouldn't see you."

"I got your message, Paula."

"Then why are you here?" she demanded.

"Because I have every intention of talking to you."

Paula kept a deadpan expression so that no trace showed of her ravaged emotions. "There's nothing left to say, Quinn. It's all been said."

"On the contrary, I have a helluva lot to say to you."

A car was approaching along the driveway, and they stepped aside to let it pass. Bertram Gideon gave Paula a wave as he drove through the archway and glanced curiously at Quinn. She wondered if her boss would have recognized who he was.

Quinn gestured to a red car that was parked at the side of the road. Not the one, her brain registered dully, he'd used before, on the weekend she'd spent at his apartment.

"How about our driving out of the village?" he suggested. "We could go someplace where we won't be interrupted."

"Why should I agree to that?"

"I'm asking you to, Paula. Surely you'll grant me that small favor."

"There'd be no point."

"We could go to the inn, if you prefer, and talk there. I know that's where you're living for now. But I didn't wait for you there because I thought you'd rather we didn't meet in front of other people."

"Am I supposed to be grateful?"

A faint smile briefly lit his eyes. "I hoped that such concern for your feelings might just open up a chink in your armor."

"Don't try to be cute with me, Quinn. I'm in no mood to be amused."

He spread his hands and shrugged. "Shall we go to the inn, then?"

Paula hesitated, wondering if she'd be a fool to agree to talk to him. Wouldn't it inevitably lead to more anguish? And yet, how could she face the rest of her life not knowing what it was that Quinn had wanted to talk to her about?

While she still hesitated, Quinn went on, "I'm a fellow guest of yours at the Woolpack. I made a reservation there just an hour ago."

Paula felt a clawing sensation of fear run the length of her spine. It would be too much to bear, knowing that Quinn was sleeping under the same roof. To have him eating in the same small dining room.

"Why are you doing this to me?" she exploded, using anger to counter her fear. "Why are you badgering me like this?"

Quinn's voice was determined but low. "I'm doing the only thing I can do, Paula. I have to get through to you somehow."

"If I agree to hear what you have to say," she said, feeling at the end of her emotional rope, "there's a condition."

"Which is?"

"That you won't stay at the Woolpack. That you'll go away afterward...right away from Barrington, I mean. This evening."

Quinn considered his answer, his eyes never leaving her face. Finally he said, "I promise to go away, Paula, if you still really want me to after you've heard me out."

"All right, then. Don't forget that you've given me your word."

They turned toward his car. Quinn's hand came up as though to take her elbow, then he let it drop again. He held the door open for Paula, but he didn't attempt to touch her again as she slid into the passenger seat.

But when Quinn was seated behind the wheel, she felt swamped by a sense of panic. This was a terrible mistake. Sitting side by side in the car, they were closed off from the rest of the world. Two people alone together . . . two people whose lovemaking had been magical. Paula's hands were resting on her lap, but she felt a compelling urge to reach out and touch him. Her fingers itched to caress the strong curves of his cheek and jawbone. She felt a strong magnetic tug that was pulling her whole body closer to his. She shut her eyes, and a tiny whimper escaped her.

"What's wrong, Paula?"

Her eyes snapped open again, and she made them focus on his face in a hostile stare.

"What's right, you might ask."

Quinn lifted his shoulders, then reached forward to switch on the ignition. Moments later they swept through the hamlet of Barrington, past the church and over the humpbacked bridge that spanned a tumbling river. The narrow road snaked steeply upward into open moorland.

"Where shall we go?" he inquired.

Paula shrugged. "Just keep driving."

"Are you enjoying working at the Barrington Museum?" he asked into the growing silence.

"Is that why you've come all this way?" she threw back with a flare of sarcasm. "To inquire if I'm happy in my new job?"

"It's a reasonable question, I'd have said."

Paula released a sigh. "I'm responsible for a unique collection of valuable porcelain. I have adequate funds at my disposal, and pretty well a free hand to do as I please. What more could I possibly want?"

Quinn swung the car onto the grassy verge, then braked and cut the engine.

"I was hoping," he said, in a quiet, neutral tone, "that you might want to marry me."

Eleven

———

Marry you?'' Paula echoed in a stunned daze.

"That's what I said."

"Are you out of your mind?"

"No, I was never saner."

"Pardon me for disagreeing," she said, her initial numbness yielding to a new flare of anger. "You must be totally insane if you think I'd consider marrying you."

"Paula, I know I said a lot of nearly unforgivable things to you, but—"

"*Nearly* unforgivable! You accused me of being the most despicable kind of cheat, you called me foul names, yet now you seem to imagine that it would be possible for me to forgive you."

"Yes, I do, Paula. I think so because of the sort of person you are."

Her heartbeat was rapid, a wild fluttering in her chest. But she kept her voice flat and unemotional. "And what sort of person am I supposed to be?"

"A wonderful person. A beautiful, warm and caring, sensitive woman."

"That's not what you thought of me before," she reminded him. "You were convinced of my guilt, Quinn. Right up until you talked to someone whose word you rated as more creditworthy than mine."

He shook his head in a gesture of self-vexation. "I wish to God I'd never talked to Sidney Crowe."

"If you hadn't talked to Sidney, you'd still believe that I played you for a sucker."

"No, I won't accept that. At first, when I was recalled to London to face charges that I'd passed on confidential information to Chamberlain's, it was like a stab in the back. I was so damned angry I couldn't begin to think straight. The fact that you'd always been so secretive about our relationship seemed to me positive proof that you were guilty. But I'd have come around eventually. You have to believe that, Paula. It tore my guts out to think you could have done something like that to me."

Paula dragged her gaze away from his and stared ahead through the windshield. They were stopped at the summit of a hill, and up here the last rays of the sinking sun still lay across the coarse grass, turning it to burnished red-gold, and leaving the valley below in a purple-misted shadow. Somehow, the melancholy beauty of the moorland scene exposed the rawness of her emotions. Tears were very close.

"What do you think it did to me?" she asked chokingly. "Did you imagine I could shrug off an accusation like that as just a little hiccup in our relationship?"

"I realize how much I hurt you," he said.

"I doubt that. I most seriously doubt that."

"Please, Paula . . . please don't be like this. You owe me a second chance."

"Owe you?" she flashed.

"Dammit, Paula, yes. You do owe me. No two people could share what we shared without having obligations to each other. You've got to listen to me. You've got to make an effort to understand my point of view."

"Like you understood mine?"

"I was wrong. Wrong all down the line. I can see it now, and that's what I'm trying to get in your head. If our relationship lacked something, and obviously it did, it was basic, instinctive trust between us. We never fully trusted each other, you and I, and we were equally guilty in that regard. For my share, I make a humble apology. I'd give an arm and a leg to wipe out the suspicions I had of you. But I'll never doubt you again, Paula, I swear it."

"It's easy to say that, Quinn, but how can you be so sure? When it comes to the crunch, you'll—"

"I can be so sure," he interrupted her, "because I know now that I love you, darling. I've loved you right from the start, I think, although I didn't recognize it as love at the time."

Paula's heart fought a raging battle with her reason. Neither came out the winner. She felt lost and floundering.

"What you call love and what I call love, Quinn, are two very different emotions."

"What do you call love, then?" he challenged, swinging in his seat to face her. "Tell me."

Paula felt thrown, curiously on the defensive. She had to grope for an answer. "It means wanting to give, wanting to share, wanting to be a part of each other's entire being. If you had loved me, truly loved me, you could never for a single second have believed I was capable of cheating you, however much the evidence seemed to point to that conclusion.''

"Maybe you're right—if it was a perfect world. But that's not the way it happened, Paula. It was *because* I loved you—even though I didn't realize it fully—that I felt so bitter. It was *because* I loved you that I called you all those vicious names. If you had been a woman who merely attracted me, a woman I'd merely had sex with, I'd just have been damned angry when I thought you'd taken me for a ride. What cut me to shreds was the belief that you— you of all the people in the world—could have done that to me. Even when I hated you the most, darling, I still loved you. I despised myself because of that. I saw it as a serious defect in my character.''

He fell silent, but Paula was still held in the grasp of his eyes. A car going by provided a momentary distraction, and she was able to break free of his mesmerizing gaze and look away.

"I do love you, Paula, I do, I do." His voice was a soft caress. "Please believe it, I do love you."

She kept her eyes averted, staring unseeingly at the windshield. The sun had gone now and the dusk was thickening around the car, enclosing the two of them even more in an intimate capsule that had no contact with the rest of the world. There was just the two of them and the powerful emotional charge that throbbed between them.

"Perhaps you do love me . . . think you love me, in your own fashion," she conceded, breaking the silence.

"Paula . . . do *you* love *me*?"

Her eyes fluttered back to meet his. "How could I love you after the horrible things you said to me?"

"But do you? That's what I asked, not how could you. *Do* you love me, Paula?"

"I did. At least . . . yes, I did."

"I want to know about now."

She gave a helpless little shake of her head. "I suppose so, in a way. It's difficult for me to give an honest answer. It all depends on what's meant by the word love."

"You just gave me your definition. On that basis, do you love me?"

She felt cornered. "It's not a matter of a simple definition. Loving embraces everything, every thought and emotion. Heart and body and soul."

"I agree. And I repeat, Paula—on that basis, do you love me?"

Her hands were trembling and she laced her fingers, gripping them tightly. She wanted to yell at Quinn, to throw her anger at him for hounding her so relentlessly.

"Yes, all right, then! If you must have me say it, I do love you. There, are you satisfied now?"

Quinn's features relaxed, the harsh, set lines of his mouth and brow instantly gone. "Thank God," he murmured huskily. "Then we can get married."

"No Quinn, that's impossible. You and I can never marry each other."

"But why in the world not? If we love each other, what possible reason can you have for holding back?"

"It just wouldn't work."

"You're crazy—of course it will work. Ours will be a fantastic marriage."

Somehow, she had to make him understand. "Listen, Quinn . . . because of our relationship, because of what's happened between us, you're in the doghouse at Sylvester's. You think I haven't heard the gossip?"

He dismissed that with an impatient gesture, but Paula insisted on having her say.

"I know you'll get back in favor at Sylvester's. You're brilliant at your job, and you'll soon start climbing the corporate ladder again. Just so long as you don't make a stupid mistake like marrying me."

"Marrying you would be no mistake, darling...."

"Yes, it would be. A stupid, reckless mistake. And you'd soon come to realize that. The slur on my reputation would inevitably rub off on you, and you'd hold me to blame for standing in the way of your career. What I say is true, Quinn, it's true."

"Even if it *were* true, darling...my career would be unimportant compared to what you and I mean to each other. Loving each other is all that matters."

Paula shook her head in forceful denial. "Just think about it, Quinn. Think hard! You're in line to succeed Lionel Fairhurst as chairman. Everybody knows it. But the top job at Sylvester's would be ruled out for you completely if you were married to me. There's no way they'll ever be totally convinced that I didn't set you up and get an advance look at their proposals for the Webberley sale. I can't let you sacrifice your whole career on my account. I just can't. And in the final analysis, you'd never be able to forgive me if I did let you."

A curious expression came over Quinn's face. "Just suppose, Paula, that I were to chuck my job at Sylvester's. What would you say then?"

"You wouldn't be such a fool."

He gave a triumphant laugh. "Too late! I've already been such a fool."

"You're not making sense," she said bemusedly.

"I wish I'd made as much sense before, sweetheart. I wish to God I'd told my associates at Sylvester's that they could damned well go to hell if they imagined I'd doubt you for a single second. I shall never be able to forgive myself for not doing just that.''

"You couldn't have known the truth then," Paula argued, not realizing that she was contradicting everything she'd said earlier. "Things did look black against me—" She broke off as understanding of what he'd just told her finally seeped through into her befuddled brain. "Are you saying that you've quit working for Sylvester's?"

"That's it, I've quit. I promised to hold the fort for them in New York until the end of this year. After that, I'll be a free man, able to decide on my own future."

"Why did you do it, Quinn?" A worried frown was clouding her brow. "Why did you take such a drastic step?"

"I had to, to put myself in the clear with you."

"But don't you see, that's just what it won't do? If I did agree to marry you now, it would only take our very first fight and you'd be regretting bitterly the brilliant career you'd given up for my sake. You're ambitious, Quinn, and . . .''

"So are you ambitious," he said. "Yet you gave up your brilliant career."

"That was different. It was done on the spur of the moment. Anyway, I'd wanted to quit Chamberlain's for a long time."

"You very nearly did quit Chamberlain's, soon after your husband died," he reminded her. "You were close to joining Sylvester's. What stopped you?"

Paula shrugged the question away. "This is hardly the time to go into that."

"I don't agree. It's exactly the time. I knew you were holding something back about that, darling, just as you were holding back about why it was so important Lady Chamberlain shouldn't get to know about the two of us.

It's my hunch that the two things are connected in some way. So out with it, Paula. I have the feeling that if you tell me about it now, it will finally clear the air between us.''

"I . . . I can't tell you."

"Yes, you can. I've admitted my mistakes to you, and I also told you the one big guilty secret of my life, remember?'' Quinn lifted his hand to her shoulder and gently fondled the lobe of her ear with his fingertips. "Now it's your turn to be totally honest with me. Do it, my love. My own sweet love. Share this problem, whatever it is."

"I can't," she whispered. "I can't."

"Tell me why you can't, then." His voice was soft and compassionate. "At least tell me what it is that's preventing you."

"Because it's not my secret," she said. "I hold it in trust. I talked about it once before, to Iain, and he betrayed me."

"I presume it was his mother he told? That doesn't take a very major step of logic."

"Yes, Iain told his mother."

Quinn's fist thumped the steering wheel in disgust. "I never did have much of an opinion of Iain Chamberlain, but it was a new low for him to go running to his mother with something that was supposed to be a confidence between him and you."

"Things weren't easy for Iain," Paula protested, surprised to find herself defending her husband. "His mother played such a dominant role in his life. His father died when he was fourteen, and from then on he depended on her for everything."

"Maybe, as a teenager. We're talking about an adult man, Paula. And, by the way, I don't much like your bracketing me with him. If Iain Chamberlain betrayed your trust, it doesn't follow that Quinn Barclay will."

"I know that, Quinn," she said contritely. "I'm sorry it seemed like that to you."

"So we're back to square one. Now let me figure this out. Your husband betrayed your confidence to his mother. After Iain died you wanted to get away from Chamberlain's—understandably—but in the end, after you'd put out feelers about joining Sylvester's, you didn't quit. I wonder why. There had to be a damn good reason. So . . . was pressure brought on you to stay, Paula? Did the redoubtable Lady C. somehow stop you from quitting?"

"She was against the idea," Paula conceded warily, disturbingly conscious of his fingers that were now caressing the nape of her neck.

"Of course she was against it. You're too darned good at your job to lose. Your joining Sylvester's would have been a major gain for them, a major loss to Chamberlain's. But how did she manage to prevent you making the switch? Answer—she had some kind of leverage, and that must have been whatever it was she learned from Iain. I'd know that it couldn't have been anything to your personal discredit, Paula, even if you hadn't already said so. It follows that you must have been protecting somebody who mattered a lot to you. Your father, right? Something your father once did that you didn't want to come out. And that old witch threatened to make it public if you quit working for her?"

"Something like that." Paula was both dismayed and impressed by his shrewd perception.

"But now you *have* quit. How come? Did you just tell her to do her worst and go to hell?"

"No, not that." She knew now that she was going to tell Quinn the whole sad story. "As a matter of fact, I retaliated in kind. I threatened her back."

Quinn's eyes grew wide with fascination. "This I have to hear. Come on, Paula—spill."

She colored faintly. "If it had been anybody else but Arabel Chamberlain I'd feel just terrible about it. You see, I told her that if she ever dared to reveal what she knew about my father, I'd confess in public to having extracted the Webberley proposals from you by trickery. And I'd implicate her by claiming that she put me up to it."

Quinn gave a short bark of laughter. "That's rich! The old girl must have been hopping mad."

"She wasn't very pleased." For the first time, the memory of that fateful confrontation brought a faint smile to Paula's lips.

"Thank the Lord," he said, "that she didn't call your bluff."

"I wasn't bluffing, Quinn."

His eyes now held tender admiration. "And I thought I was tough! But underneath you're as soft as butter. That's what I love about you. Correction! I love everything about you, darling. The complete Paula package."

She felt intensely moved as he reached for her hand and held it between both of his. Quinn was telling her that whatever she had to confide would make no difference to his love for her.

"I was very close to my father," she began. "I guess that's inevitable, when one parent dies young and you're an only child. Like you with your mother. And Iain with his mother, too, I suppose. Anyway, I hero-worshipped my dad; he was everything that was good and wonderful in my eyes. It went on that way right up until his last illness. Dad was in the hospital, so I stepped in and tried to keep things running for him. It was during the university long vacation and I was home, anyway. One day, I was going through a mountain of papers and trying to make sense out of the muddle.... Dad was never very organized. I came across a page ripped from a notebook that mystified me. It had various hieroglyphics on it that I couldn't decipher, but I figured out enough to realize that something was very wrong. When I asked Dad about those notes he wouldn't tell me anything at first, but then it all came out. They referred to a Renoir painting that had passed through his hands a couple of years before, but it was a sale that hadn't been recorded in his books. The problem was that he'd bought that painting from Fritz Mullen."

"Mullen? Oh, my God!"

"It was just a few days before Fritz Mullen was arrested for the forgery of a number of French Impressionist paintings, including several Renoirs. My father was stunned. He said it was a magnificent picture, rather like *The Swing*, with lovely soft colors and lots of dappled sunlight. He just couldn't believe it was a forgery. And yet it had come to him from Mullen. So Dad removed some flakes of paint and threads of canvas from one corner and analyzed them."

"And the results were what you'd found scribbled on that piece of paper?"

Paula nodded. "They proved conclusively, of course, that the painting was a modern forgery."

"So what did your father do?"

"He just didn't know what to do. Fritz Mullen was heading for a jail sentence, and if my father had told the police about the fake Renoir he'd bought, he'd have stood no chance of getting back the enormous sum of money he'd paid for it. So, after much heart searching, he sold it as a genuine Renoir."

"And it never came to light?" Quinn asked in wonderment. "Who did he sell it to?"

"I don't know. Some foreign buyer, but Dad just wouldn't tell me who. He said it was better that I didn't know, because then I wouldn't ever feel that I had to do anything about it. He said that the buyer was a very rich man, and that he'd get an enormous amount of pleasure out of owning the painting, which really was a beautiful picture. And he also told me that he didn't think there was much risk of it coming to light that it wasn't a genuine Renoir—at least not for a long time. I think my father chose the buyer very carefully, Quinn—partly to be safe, of course, but partly to salve his conscience."

"But what about the provenance? How did he manage about that? A mention of Fritz Mullen's name on the documentation would have killed the deal stone dead."

"Dad had to forge the documentation," Paula said in a small voice. "That was what was so awful. He'd bought the picture in good faith, believing that he could make a reasonable profit on the deal, and if he'd sold it at once he'd have been morally in the clear. But he hung on to the painting longer than he normally would have done, *because* it was so lovely. He enjoyed having it in his possession for a little while. And then, when the Fritz Mullen case broke, he faced utter ruin."

She met Quinn's eyes with a look that pleaded for his understanding. "It wasn't for himself Dad did this, it was for me. I was about to start at university at that time, and it would be several years before I stopped being financially dependent on him. Of course, if I'd known what Dad was planning, I'd have told him not to do it. I wouldn't have wanted my education to be bought at such a terrible cost. But I didn't know, Quinn . . . I didn't know until long afterward, when it was too late to change anything."

Quinn gave a wry smile. "It's a strange ethical problem, isn't it? The only intrinsic value a painting has is what somebody, somewhere, is willing to pay for it. And what's that figure based on? When it comes to the big-league stuff, it's nothing more than the belief that a painting is genuinely the work of a certain famous artist whose reputation has pushed up the selling price. A beautiful painting by Fritz Mullen, Tom Keating or Elmyr de Hory is still a beautiful painting. But it isn't worth a fraction of what that same painting would cost if it were a genuine Renoir or Constable or whoever. It doesn't make a lot of sense, does it?" Quinn's arm had slipped to lie across her shoulders. He kept his fingers still now, just comforting her with his tender warmth. "Don't quote me, for God's sake, but I have to admit to having a secret admiration for Mullen and his ilk. It must be galling for them to be unable to sell their own work for much more than peanuts, but find that what they paint in the guise of another man's work is revered as a masterpiece of the highest order. Still, no amount of philosophizing will change things. If you're in the art world, you have to play by the art world's rules."

Paula nodded her head sadly. "My father had to live the rest of his life—what little remained of it—with the knowledge that he was a crook. That was his own name for himself. A crook! In retrospect, I can see what it cost him in self-esteem. He was a changed man in those last couple of years. All the zest had gone, all the fun. I'd merely thought he was getting older and more tired. But then, just before his death, I discovered the true reason for the change."

"Poor Paula!" Quinn's arms were wrapped around her and he held her close. Paula found it wonderfully solacing, and she rested her head against his shoulder, nuzzling her face into his neck.

"It didn't make me love Dad any the less," she whispered, "but I couldn't help being...resentful. And I resented what he'd done even more when it put me at Arabel Chamberlain's mercy."

"I understand, darling, I understand. But you've finally got that old witch off your back. Now you just have to shake off that other person who's been hounding you."

Paula glanced up at him. "Other person?"

"You. You, yourself." A hand lifted to caress her cheek. "You seem to think that in some obscure way you're responsible for your father's transgression. But that's a screwy idea. A crime was perpetrated, and there's nothing you can do about righting it. Ralph Grayson was obviously a basically honest man, a loving and lovable man. Cling to all the wonderful memories you have of him, darling, and jettison everything else. Forget it."

She shook her head. "I can't, Quinn. I can't help remembering that my education was bought with illicit money."

"So what d'you want to do? Cancel out your education? That's an impossibility, and even if it were possible, it would be wrong. All the talent and knowledge you have locked up in your brain, sweetheart, doesn't just belong to you. It belongs to the rest of the world."

"I suppose so."

"I know so. Trust me."

Paula felt a strange sense of peace and calm seeping through her veins. Telling Quinn was something she should have done weeks ago. She should have trusted him from the very start, as her heart had urged her to. She knew now that, as time went by, her father's single lapse would slot into its proper place in her memory, no longer assuming the inflated proportions that Arabel's blackmail had given it.

They sat on in harmonious silence. Paula was aware that Quinn was giving her time to adjust her mind and come to terms with the new situation. The last trace of crimson had faded from the sky. Above them, stars were beginning to show, pinpricks in the bluey blackness. Below, the misted valley had its own faint stars, the lights of the village and the museum.

Finally Quinn stirred. She felt the grip of his fingers on her shoulders as he drew her around to face him.

"Paula, darling Paula. You know that I love you, don't you?"

"Oh, Quinn, I love you, too. I love you so much."

They kissed, gently, almost experimentally. It was putting a seal on the past, setting a promise for the future. The passing seconds stretched to minutes, and their murmured endearments grew less coherent. Then Paula surfaced enough to say, sighing, "What are we going to do, Quinn?"

"Get married, of course. At once or sooner."

"Of course get married," she scoffed. "You don't imagine I'd let you escape me now? I didn't mean that at all. What are we going to do about our jobs, our careers?"

"So we're down to the secondary considerations." Quinn touched tiny kisses to her face. "I have all that figured out."

"Without consulting me?"

"I meant," he amended, in a chastened voice, "I have some suggestions to make on the subject."

"Let's hear them."

"What we've both of us been doing up until now," he expounded, "was working for the continuance of existing dynasties. I think it's time we laid the foundations for a dynasty of our own."

"Set up in business together, you mean?" The thought excited her; anything in partnership with Quinn would have excited her. "What have you in mind?"

"Antiques auctioneering, naturally. It's what we're both best at. Our combined skills will be formidable."

"Starting from scratch, Quinn, it'll be a long haul."

"Does that thought deter you?"

She considered the point and smiled. "Why should it? We have plenty of time ahead of us to reach success."

"What do we call our new company?"

"Barclay's, what else? Barclay's Fine Art Auctioneers."

She pondered a moment. "Quinn, I have to finish out my six months at the Barrington. That's my contract."

"And I have to be in New York until Christmas. But I flatly refuse to go more than ten days at a stretch without holding you in my arms. That's the absolute limit of my endurance."

"The airlines are going to do well out of us."

"I'll get to know each wave on the Atlantic. And by the way, talking about endurance, isn't it time we were moving?"

Paula laughed, sloughing off some of her tension. "Hungry already? I always knew you were greedy."

"That's me. You're about to find out just how greedy."

She shivered as his mouth trailed a sensuous pathway around her face, shivered even more enjoyably as his tongue tip probed the contours of her ear.

"I just hope you haven't any fancy ideas about the kind of food served at the Woolpack," she intoned, struggling to keep a hold on her sanity. "Good, plain, country fare is what you'll get for your supper."

"Supper," he said, "will come later. Much later."

"Oh, you mean *that* sort of greedy?"

"As if you didn't know. Do you have a nice bedroom? What's it like?"

"Why should I waste my breath telling you, since it looks as if you're about to see it for yourself?"

"You bet! Not that I expect to take much notice of the decor."

"The bed," she said, "is a huge brass-knobbed affair. It has an old-fashioned feather mattress that's billowy soft."

"So we're about to make love on a feather mattress."

"It'll be like floating on a cloud," she said dreamily.

"Floating on a cloud is for fantasy time. This is going to be for real, Paula, my darling. For real and for always."

Quinn turned the ignition key and the engine sprang to life. He made the slickest three-point turn there ever was, and then they were racing down the hill as if five seconds was too long to wait for the new beginning that beckoned them.

Silhouette Desire

DECEMBER TITLES

LOVEPLAY
Diana Palmer

FIRESTORM
Doreen Owens Malek

JULIET
Ashley Summers

SECRET LOVE
Nancy John

FOOLISH PLEASURE
Jennifer Greene

TEXAS GOLD
Joan Hohl

Silhouette Desire

COMING NEXT MONTH

TREASURE HUNT
Maura Seger

Lucas didn't want to take Emily with him on the dive, he found her more distracting than any woman had a right to be. Worse still, somewhere between eluding the modern-day pirates and recovering the sunken diamonds, Lucas discovered that he had fallen for her.

THE MYTH AND THE MAGIC
Christine Flynn

When a mysterious fossilized skeleton was unearthed in Stephanie's yard a team of paleontologists arrived to poke around in the mud. Enter Dr. Adam Colter — rugged, handsome. Unfortunately, the combination of Stephanie's impulsiveness and Adam's scientific logic seemed to mean nothing but trouble.

LOVE UNDERCOVER
Sandra Kleinschmit

Investigative reporter Brittany Daniels wanted a story, police detective Gabe Spencer was after a criminal. Brittany had no objections to working with him undercover but Gabe was harder to convince. However, even his objections began to crumble when he saw how well Brittany played the role of a gangster's moll…

COMING NEXT MONTH

SERENDIPITY SAMANTHA
Jo Ann Algermissen

Samantha was smugly certain that one ride in her
temperamental car, one gourmet dinner of peanut
butter and jelly and one *long* visit to her "when's the
wedding?" parents would send Jack Martin
running. She was an inventor, she had no time for
desire — did she?

MOMENT OF TRUTH
Suzanne Simms

Alex took one look at his pinstripes and knew that
Kincaid definitely was *not* for her. So what made her
think that behind those too-serious gray-green eyes
and that too-rare smile she saw a flash of
something…wild? Why did his kiss have such a
devastating effect on her?

DESTINY'S DAUGHTER
Elaine Camp

Years before, Banner's mother had deserted her
family for the love of another man. Yuri was that
man's son. His love made Banner want to live a new,
exciting life, but would the past that they couldn't
control destroy their chance for a future?

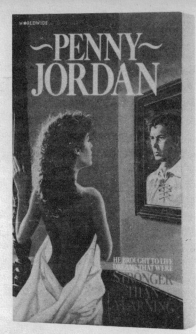

Bewitched in her dreams she awoke to discover the face of reality

The same dark hair, the same mocking eyes. The Regency rake in the portrait, the seducer of Jenna's dreams had a living double.

But James Allingham was no dream, he was a direct descendant of the black sheep of the Deveril family.

They would fight for the possession of the ancestral home. They would fight against desire to be together.

Unravel the mysteries in
STRONGER THAN YEARNING,
a new longer romance from
Penny Jordan.